CW01024547

WHEN THE TIME COMES

JOSEF WINKLER

Selected Other Works by
Josef Winkler

Mutter und der Bleistift

Wortschatz der Nacht

Roppongi: Requiem für einen Vater

Natura Morta

Domra, am Ufer des Ganges

Friedhof der bitteren Orangen

Die Verschleppung

Das wilde Kärnten

In English Translation

Flowers for Jean Genet

The Serf

WHEN THE TIME COMES

JOSEF WINKLER

TRANSLATED BY

ADRIAN WEST

First Contra Mundum Press edition 2013.

Originally published in German as *Wenn es soweit ist – Erzählung* in 1998.

Library of Congress
Cataloguing-in-Publication Data

Winkler, Josef, 1953–

[Wenn es soweit ist – Erzählung.
English.]

When the Time Comes / Josef Winkler;
Translated from the original German by Adrian West;
introduction by Adrian West.

—1st Contra Mundum Press
Edition
228 pp., 5x8 in.

ISBN 9781940625010

I. Winkler, Josef.
II. Title.
III. West, Adrian.
IV. Translator.
V. West, Adrian.
VI. Introduction.

2013948951

INTRODUCTION

Josef Winkler was born in Kamering, a small farming village in the mountains of Austria's southernmost province of Carinthia, a mostly rural area slightly smaller than Los Angeles County that has given birth to a long list of writers of international stature, among them Robert Musil, Ingeborg Bachmann, and Peter Handke. His father, the Plowman, as he calls him in other works, with reference to the dialogue between Death and the Plowman by the Medieval German writer Johannes von Tepl, seems to have devoted himself single-mindedly to his estate, his crops, and his livestock, showing little regard for his bookish, anemic son, to whom he would one day bellow, as the novel *Roppongi* recounts: "When I'm no longer around, I do not want you to come to my funeral." Among the few phrases he attributes to his mother, who was left speechless by the deaths of her three brothers in the Second World War, & whose desolate resignation is the subject of Winkler's most recent work, *Mutter und der Bleistift*, is the admonition: "We've got no money for books!"

Thus, as is so frequently the case in Austrian literature, his writing is a writing-against: a deflation of the clichés of pastoralism, an unveiling of the cruelty and corruption moldering beneath the serenity of the alpine countryside, and a reprisal on behalf of the neglected and repressed against that nation's "Catholic National Socialist spirit ... which is in fact a negation of the spirit," in the words of Thomas Bernhard. His vehemence has carried over into his articles in the popular press, where he has been ruthless in his attacks on the venality of the Austrian political establishment. Yet in spite of his well-known intransigence, the label of *Nestbeschmutzer* or gadfly hardly exhausts the range of his work.

Winkler's autobiographical novels, based on true events and incorporating living persons, skirt the outer limits of the genre: their art lies not in the fabrication of scenarios, but in a painstaking rendering of visual detail and an attention to the musicality of phrases that often extend over entire pages. His approach is the precise opposite of the fervor for novelty characteristic of so much of contemporary literary culture, where authors become brands and must keep current through an increasingly perverse prostration to the whims of the literary market or risk their work's being remaindered and forgotten: in general, his books are meditations on the same limited number of motifs from his childhood and youth, seen now from one angle, now from another, picked up, caressed, and set back down repeatedly, like the tatter of rope that sits on the desk of Maximilian in the present novel, having previously held the bodies of the suicides Jonathan and Leopold dangling over the floor of the parish house barn.

When the Time Comes is Josef Winkler's ninth book. Many of the events it examines — the aforementioned double suicide, the drowning of the maidservant who paints her face with menstrual blood, or the author's aunt holding him over his grandmother's coffin and enjoining him to look down at the lifeless face below — appear in his earlier novels as well, particularly in the trilogy *Das wilde Kärnten.* "Death," Winkler has said, "is my life's theme." There can therefore be no question of *moving on,* as the cliché goes. "I am happy," he says elsewhere, "among the dead, they do me no harm, & they are people as well." Winkler often gives the impression of being alive only reluctantly, by compulsion or in deference to others, and seems even to resent the vitality that separates him from the cadavers that haunt his dreams.

If the characters and incidents related in *When the Time Comes* are not new in Winkler's work, their treatment here is nonetheless unique. Less novel than poem, it revolves around the central metaphor of the bone cooker who brews a black stock that is painted on the horses of the farmers in the village to ward off insects: the bone cooker becomes the chronicler of the village's dead, recounting the story of their disastrous ends before laying their skeletons in a clay vessel, one atop the other. His ominous narration is interlaced with verses from

Catholic songbooks and the stanzas of Baudelaire's "Litanies of Satan," and follows an architectural motif based on the cruciform village of Pulsnitz, at the center of which lies a calvary where a painting by the parish priest, depicting a sinner laid out in torment on the floor of Hell, consigns the residents to their doom. Like Homer in the Catalogue of Ships or the Trojan Battle Order, Winkler enumerates the bloodlines of the benighted families that populate the town, their relations devoid of warmth and serving only to pass on the inheritance of extinction. As Thomas Wirtz comments, reviewing the book for the *Frankfurter Allgemeine Zeitung*, "Winkler's genealogies are forced death institutions." Carinthia comes to be seen as a kind of House of Atreus writ large, its inexorable decadence symptomatic both of the suffering and solitude of the author's childhood and of the longing for symbolic vengeance thereby inspired.

My first encounter with Winkler's work was in 2011, when I purchased a pair of books that had been issued by Ariadne Press some fifteen years before: his fourth novel, *The Serf*, and the short meditation *Flowers for Jean Genet*, translated by Michæl Mitchell & Michæl Roloff respectively. The first, composed after a long absence from his home village, is a reframing of the tale of the prodigal son inspired by the words of the baroque dramatist Jakob Ayrer: "I am the serf of death / It cannot but be so." The second is representative of a type of narrative Winkler would return to in *Domra: am Ufer des Ganges*, and the astonishing book of short fiction, *Ich reiß mir eine Wimper aus und stech dich damit tot*, a hybrid of travel writing & capsule biography in which Winkler examines foreign landscapes through the lens of his totem writers and the recollections their words dredge up. These books impressed me deeply: only rarely does one encounter an artistic vision of such singularity married to a style so elegantly wrought and resolute; and I was dismayed to find, after I had finished them, that nothing had been translated into English since, nor anything written save the odd scant reference in surveys of German-language literature, an academic article or two, & a single book review in *World Literature Today*; a fact that, while much to the credit of the latter publication, highlights the dismal but widespread tendency to emphasize the exoticism of the allegedly foreign at the expense of its individual æsthetic virtues, so that the reading of writers from beyond the Anglo-American sphere comes to be seen at best as a curious diversion, like *ethnic* cuisine, and at worst as an obligation to qualify for that most contemptible of modern virtues, *well-roundedness*.

Josef Winkler's standing in the German-speaking literary world is beyond question: from the Special Jury Award at the 1979 Ingeborg Bachmann Prize for excerpts from his second novel to his recent election as President of the Austrian Arts Senate, his career has comprised an uninterrupted succession of accolades & recognitions, the most notable of which was his being presented with the Büchner Prize in 2008. His writing has been acclaimed by the eminent critic Marcel Reich-Ranicki, by W.G. Sebald, by the Nobel Prize winners Elfriede Jelinek & Günter Grass. For these reasons alone, his near-absence in the literary consciousness of English-speaking readers strikes me as unconscionable. It was with the wish of remedying this omission that I began to translate Winkler's work in the spring of 2012, at first with short pieces in *Asymptote* and *Jwriction: Review,* and then with a serialization of the present text, in a somewhat different version, in the *Brooklyn Rail.* As more publications followed, it became clear that there was a broad interest in seeing more of Winkler in print & that, thanks in part to the wave of independent presses willing to take risks to shed light on underrepresented writers, and in part to the communication among readers facilitated by such online outlets as *3:AM, Words Without Borders,* and *The Quarterly Conversation,* the audience for fiction in translation had grown immeasurably in the decade and a half since Winkler's first appearance in English.

For me, the importance of Josef Winkler lies in his radical insistence on the priority of lived experience against the allegedly artistic, but actually merely commercial, imperative to innovation; not to mention his categorical refusal of decorum or compromise. There are stories that Winkler has told a dozen times in his books; but these stories are never over, he stresses, their figures will not stay in their graves, and we are wrong to try to push them away. Not only does one have the sense, in Winkler's work, that there is something morally higher than the esthetic proscription of repetitiousness; we also feel that his concern for the effects of obsession on the course of a life — he has now been writing for thirty-five years, without ever averting his gaze from the catastrophes of his Carinthian childhood — is something nearly unprecedented in scope and originality.

WHEN THE TIME COMES

The bone stock, said the ninety-year-old man with the gray-flecked moustache and the trimmed eyebrows, was brewed in the village by a little man who lived in miserable circumstances. He used to gather up the bones from the slaughter and lay them in a clay vessel, which he placed in a hole in the ground over glowing coals and covered up with dirt & clumps of grass. He would let the bones simmer down to a greasy, viscous brew, called "Pandapigl" in the dialect of Carinthia. The bone cooker would wrap the small smoking furnace made of boards in barbed wire, and he had it guarded by a dog that crouched there day and night. From time to time, as a child, the now ninety-year-old man would take an empty beer bottle to the bone cooker and have him fill it with the bone stock and pay him a few cents, or in kind, with a bit of meat, sausage, bread or milk. Amid the heat of summer, the farm people would take a crow's feather and smear the dense, black liquid on the horse that pulled the hay cart, around the eyes and in the outer ears, and on the nostrils and the belly, because the putrid-smelling stock warded off the insects that used to pester the cart horses, above all on the hot summer days, so vexing them at times that they would take off through the fields, kicking and jerking their heads, and crash with their carriages on the shores of the Drava.

"Let us note in passing that the Christian's attitude in prayer, head and eyes lowered, is unfa-
vorable to meditation. It is a posture conducive
to a closed and submissive intellectual disposi-
tion, & it discourages spiritual audacity. If you
choose this position, God may come, swoop
down on the nape of your neck, and leave his
mark there, where it may linger a long time. In
order to meditate, you must find an open attitude
— not defiant — but not prostrate before God.
You must proceed cautiously. A bit too much sub-
mission & God will bestow his grace upon you:
then you're fucked."

IN THE VERY BOTTOM of the clay vessel where the putrid-smelling bone stock was rendered from the bones of slaughtered animals, to be brushed on the horses with a crow's feather around the eyes, on the ears and nostrils, and on their bellies, to protect them from the flies, the horseflies, & mosquitoes, lie the arm bones of a man, torn from his body in a trench on the battlefield, who dragged a life-sized statue of Jesus through the forest before the Second World War and threw it over a waterfall. Even after days of searching, they couldn't find Jesus' arms, broken off from his body in the fall — the pastor, Balthasar Kranabeter, wandered for nights on end through the forest, with a flashlight and a prayer card hanging around his neck, praying loudly Holy God, we praise thy name, Lord of all, we bow before thee — but in retribution, according to the priest, the blasphemer lost his own arms in Hitler's war, spent the rest of his days with a wooden prosthesis to which iron hooks were affixed, and had to be fed by his wife and children. Before meals, he would make the sign of the cross over his forehead, lips, and breast with the iron hooks affixed to his prosthesis, and pray, Come, Lord Jesus, be our guest, and bless what thou hast bestowed. Since then, the village priest & painter of prayer cards used to say, lifting his index finger menacingly before the wide eyes of the children of the landowners and peasants seated before him for their religion lessons, that town built in the form of a cross, which had already been burned to the ground at the turn of the century, is encaged in an image framed left to right, top to bottom, by fire, and the profaner of Christ lies within it, his hands aloft among the red and yellow flames darting upward from the floor of Hell, his naked torso bound by a green serpent as thick as a man's arm. Red-winged Lucifer leans over the sinner and spills a cup of gall into his mouth. *Ô toi, le plus savant et le plus beau des Anges, Dieu trahi par le sort et privé de louanges, Ô Satan, prends pitié de ma longue misère!*

WITH THE STATUE of Saint George, patron saint of horses, which was brushed in the early morning, while the dewdrops still glistened on the periwinkles growing along the church's outer wall, with the black bone stock, smelling of decay, around the eyes, nose, mouth, and halo, the townspeople, among them Maximilian's then eight-year-old father, walked the four kilometers from Pulsnitz to Großbotenfeld at seven in the morning, led by the sacristan carrying a cross. With the life-sized statue borne by four men, the faithful would take the outstretched right arm of the village rebuilt in the form of a cross — fifteen years before, some children playing with fire had reduced it to ashes — and slip between the cramped fingers of the crucified right hand, praying their Hail Marys and Our Fathers until they had passed over the palm pierced by the nail and then falling quiet as they arrived at the dank Ponta forest, where to this day thousands of snowdrops still blossom in the springtime. The Ponta forest was also called Galgenbichl, where the criminals were hanged, Maximilian's ninety-year-old father said, and as a child, when he would go on foot to Kindelbrücken to take a message to his grandfather or bring him his mail, he used to pass by there as quickly as possible, in dread. The murmuring of the procession only rose again when the pilgrims had turned toward the neighboring township of Nußbach, likewise built in the form of a cross, and had left the Galgenbichl behind. After a mass held in a clover field in Großbotenfeld, paid for year after year by Maximilian's grandfather, Florian Kirchheimer, a horse-breeder esteemed far & wide, the Saint George procession would disband. The pilgrims visited their friends and family, the taste of the host still in their mouths, or went to the inn, or sauntered home on the field and forest paths. The statue was lifted onto a calash and pulled back to Pulsnitz, where it took up its place in the church, by two horses accompanied by the priest and Maximilian's grandfather, and running girls would follow behind them, daisy wreaths woven with horsehair into their hair. *Let the scent of this sacrifice rise to thee, Lord, and our words not be ignored. We have slain not calves, but thy sacred heir, who shall lead us away from despair.*

IN THE CLAY VESSEL where the pandapigl was rendered, to be brushed on the horses with a crow's feather around the eyes and nostrils and on the belly, to protect them from mosquitoes and horseflies, Maximilian, the bone collector, lays atop the arm bones of the blasphemer, who threw a life-sized statue of Jesus over a waterfall before the Second World War and lost his own arms on the battlefield — That was a punishment from God! the priest would scream over and over from the pulpit —, the bones of his great-grandmother, Paula Rosenfelder, who lost a son in the First World War and took her own life, it was said, because she feared her pregnant daughter, who lay in bed with an infection, would fall ill with the Spanish flu and succumb to death, as so many other young women in the village built in the form of a cross had done. Her husband, August Rosenfelder, Maximilian's great-grandfather, came back home from the cattle market, looked for his wife in the kitchen and stable, went into his pregnant daughter's bedroom & asked after her mother. Throwing the quilt back from over her head, his flu-sick daughter whispered hoarsely: She's gone back up to the attic! The bone collector's great-grandfather climbed the steep attic staircase and saw, before he had reached the last step, his wife's head hanging modestly over her breast. He approached the corpse, strangled with a calf halter, and cried: But mama! But mama! It seems Maximilian's grandmother, Leopoldine Felsberger, pregnant with Maximilian's uncle, Kajetan Felsberger, at the time of her mother's suicide, kept the incident long concealed, and only spoke of it during the Second World War, after hearing that her son Michæl — the third to have done so — had fallen in Russia, in the vicinity of Nevel. She fainted in the garden and was carried into the house by her husband, his legs quivering. When she came to, she lit a candle and prayed more than an hour for the souls of her three fallen sons, & then, in tears, she told of her mother's suicide for the first time.

August Rosenfelder, Maximilian's alcoholic great-grandfather, was often mocked and jeered at by the fourteen-year-old Rupert, a schoolmate of the now ninety-year-old man with the gray-flecked moustache and the trimmed eyebrows. When the young man had once again aped his bandy-legged gait, the drunk struck him in the face with a switch of hazelnut. The fourteen-year-old stood crying with a broken nose and blood-smeared face before the shouting old man brandishing his switch. His daughter-in-law, who wanted to limit his alcohol intake, filled his empty schnapps bottle with bleach. The bleach corroded his throat and pharynx so badly that he could hardly nourish himself and only ate and drank with unbearable pain. In his eighty-first year, soon after this grievous injury, he tied a black rosary around his wrist, went into the stable, unfastened the hemp cord from one of the calves crouched at the feeding trough, wound the rope around his neck and hanged himself from the doorframe of the stable.

In the clay vessel-where the putrid-smelling bone stock was rendered from the bones of slaughtered animals, to be painted on the horses with a crow's feather in the summer heat, around the eyes and nostrils and on the belly, to protect them from the pricking and blood-sucking horseflies and mosquitoes, lies the skeleton of the hanged August Rosenfelder over the skeleton of his wife Paula, who took her life up in the attic. A thick black braid covered her right eye and the tip of her tongue, which stuck out from between her lips. When the stable doors were forced open, his hobnailed shoes clacked against the wooden floor, and the rosary swung back and forth between the blue tips of his contracted fingers, and the young woman, who had been looking for her father-in-law, and who had burned out his esophagus with bleach, felt the burst of the stall air and saw her father-in-law dangling in the dung-splattered doorway, his tongue protruding from his mouth. *I hear a call ring out: Brother! wake from thy slumber, the Lord is come to us, night is far, the day is nigh! Eschew all deeds borne of the night! Henceforth may all men bear the arms of light!*

THE FIFTEEN-YEAR-OLD LUDMILLA FELFERNIG, Maximilian's mother said, had to work on the Schaflechner farm with peasants and menials who mocked and jeered at her incessantly. Once, the boys were stacking straw bales on the threshing floor of the barn when the girl, to use his mother's words, became unwell. As she bent over the straw bales, the boys made fun of the blood that had seeped through her underwear. In tears, the girl let the straw bale fall and ran down the gangway of the hayloft and down the village street to the calvary, where she knelt, folding her hands in prayer, under the flames leaping up from the floor of Hell. While the menstrual blood ran over her thighs, she sobbed out, with a pounding heart: Angel of God, my guardian dear, to whom His love entrusts me here, ever this day be at my side, to light and guard, to rule and guide. Wedging her hand between her thighs, she smeared blood on her face, on the whitewashed wall of the calvary, and on the devil's horned head, & ran, red-masked, with blood-drenched hands and thighs, past the graveyard, where the crosses stood stiff as life-sized toy soldiers, stretching their thorn-crowned heads, past the church, over the slope of the pond, down through fields fenced in with rusted barbed wire hung with tufts of gray and brown hair from the grazing cattle, through the narrow, tangled woodlands by the river, and flung herself into the rapids of the Drava. After days of pointless searching, her corpse was pulled out of the river in Villach. Milla got snagged up in the grating on the Drava bridge! Thus Maximilian's mother, the wife of the ninety-year-old man with the gray-flecked moustache and the trimmed eyebrows.

In the clay vessel where the pandapigl was rendered from the bones of slaughtered animals, to be painted on the horses with a crow's feather, around the eyes and nostrils and on the belly, to protect them from the pestering mosquitoes & horseflies, the bone collector lays the skeleton of the fifteen-year-old girl, found caught up among the driftwood in the grating and pulled up out of the river, over the skeleton of August Rosenfelder, whose dung-splattered corpse was cut down from the stable door before the cow tails swinging back and forth. Opposite the schoolhouse, in the center of the town built in the form of a cross, in front of the calvary where the blasphemer, who threw the life-sized Jesus over a cliff, lies among the flames of Hell, holding his hands aloft, while Lucifer, his red wings unfurled, bends over his victim, to spill a cup of gall in his open mouth while he cries out in misery, the funeral train halted, with the black-clothed priest, the acolytes in black & white, the peasants and menials bearing lit candles and murmuring prayers. With holy water and incense, the priest blessed the bloody handprints the young suicide had left on the walls of the calvary and on the image of Hell that he himself had painted, saying: *Ô Prince de l'exil, à qui l'on a fait tort, Et qui, vaincu, toujours te redresses plus fort, Ô Satan, prends pitié de ma longue misère!*

IN THE DEPTHS OF WINTER, at twenty degrees below zero, when Maximilian's grandfather Florian Kirchheimer used to drive the horse-sleigh laden with milk cans twenty kilometers among the snowdrifts from Pulsnitz to the dairy in Villach, he would put on an ankle-length leather coat with a tufted black lamb's wool liner. For the townspeople, who sent their milk over to the dairy, he was given raw sugar & oil in exchange; wrapped to his ankles in his leather coat, his sleigh hung with icicles, he would pass them out to the townspeople on his return in the same place where he'd picked up the milk. He would draw the oil up out of a jerry can and pour it into glass bottles carried by the townspeople who stood there waiting for him.

Maximilian's father, the ninety-year-old man with the gray-flecked moustache and the trimmed eyebrows, said that as a child of five, afflicted with a severe inflammation of the middle ear, he had sat one winter day in the horse-sleigh beside his father in his ankle-length leather coat with the tufted black sheep's wool liner, a wool scarf wrapped around his head to protect his aching ears, while they carted logs held together by heavy iron chains from Römerhof to Frankenhausen by way of Pulsnitz. While his father was handing over the logs at the sawmill in Frankenhausen — from afar you could hear the blows of the pickaxes against the tree trunks, round, moist, & slippery, crashing against one another as they were dragged from the horse-sleigh — the five-year-old child, suffering from an inflammation of the middle ear, was treated in the office of Doctor Lamprecht.

For a sick call, the bone collector's father said, you had to seek out the country doctor, in winter with the horse-sleigh and in summer in a calash. Only later did the doctor buy himself a horse and ride out to see the sick and dying. Before harnessing the nag in the summer heat and mounting its shimmering flanks with his brown leather doctor's bag, he would brush the black bone stock, smelling of decay, around the horse's eyes & nostrils, on its outer ears and on its belly, with a crow's feather, to drive away the insects.

On the way back to Pulsnitz from Frankenhausen, the child of five with his head bound up sat again in the horse-sleigh beside his father, who grasped the cracking leather reigns, clothed in an ankle-length leather coat lined in tufted black sheep's wool; moaning low to stifle the pain in his ears, he watched the two horses trotting along the spruce forest's edge, the silvery glimmer of their hooves in the sun. The reigns still hang today, the leather dark gray, worn thin by the horses' hindquarters and now cracked and peeling, along with the rusty harness, in the attic of Maximilian's parents' house, under wasps' nests the size of soccer balls.

As a twelve-year-old child, Maximilian's father shoved a hay bale into the chaff cutter in the hayloft. Before the boy could pull his hand back, his brother Eduard spun the wheel of the machine in a circle and cut off one of the child's fingers with the rotary blade. The two brothers ran screaming down the gangway, the younger one holding his right hand in the air, its little finger hanging by a flap of skin, and into their parents' house. The village midwife, lingering in the kitchen & chatting with Maximilian's great-grandmother about the floral decorations for the high altar on the coming Corpus Christi, cut the flap of skin with a pair of scissors and threw the child's finger on the dung heap, where it landed among the roosters and hens, which jerked their heads, cackling in fright, and scratched at the ground. After the midwife had disinfected the child's stump, she smeared a black and bitter-smelling ointment on it, tied a piece of cloth over the wound with a white thread, and washed the blood from his forearm. The mother assembled her six children around the table and lit a candle. The children folded their hands — coarse, chapped, and filthy, the nails chewed away — and prayed to their guardian angel, staring fixedly at the candle's wavering yellow flame.

For two whole summers, when he was five and six, Maximilian's father had lived with his asthmatic grandmother, who was sent to recuperate in a little roadside cabin overlooking a brook in the mountains in Innerkrems, where thousands of sheep, cows, and horses grazed in the pastures. His grandmother would buy polenta and milk from the neighboring farm people and make breakfast and dinner for herself and her grandson at the open hearth. From time to time, his father Florian rode a horse — a bottle of the black bone stock lay near to hand in his saddlebag — the forty kilometers to Innerkrems & brought his son home-baked bread, speck, sausage and potatoes. As classes had already begun in his hometown of Pulsnitz, the six-year-old went to school in Innerkrems for a time. Between his teeth you could still see the yellow grains of polenta as the ninety-year-old man with the gray-flecked moustache & trimmed eyebrows grinned, bright-eyed, and told of how the teacher in Innerkrems, from whom he had learned his first letters, used to ride to school on a white horse, trailed by shouting children.

AMONG THE GREEN GRASSHOPPERS leaping left and right, forward and backward like sparklers over his shoes, the boy used to go often in the midday summer heat, through the meadows smelling of herbs and fresh-cut grass, or in the fall through the misted-over fields of stubble, when the black, mildew-scented leaves from the bushes growing on the forest's edge clung to the bottoms of his hobnailed shoes, but also in the knee-deep new snow or the iced-over fields — the deer would sink down in the snow, their long slender legs breaking through the crust that glimmered in the sunlight — to Kindelbrücken, where his grandfather, Ferdinand Kirchheimer, lived in the Buggelsheim Inn, to bring him a message or his mail. The grandfather would give the child a slice of Reinling with cinnamon-coated raisins baked in, spreading yellow butter and his hand-harvested honey on the pastry. Eat, boy! Eat! He would say as the honey dripped off the bread and ran between the boy's fingers. The boy would lick the honey from his fingers, eating one slice of Reinling after another at his grandfather's side while the latter opened letters and sipped coffee. He observed the old man's gray beard hair by hair. I can still remember his coffee cup very well, it was white, had blue dots, and a dark blue lip. The enamel was chipped in several places: thus Maximilian's ninety-year-old father. When his grandfather died — his skeleton lies in the clay vessel where the bone stock was rendered from the bones of slaughtered animals, to be brushed on the horses with a crow's feather, around the eyes & nostrils and on the belly, to protect them from the bloodsucking mosquitoes and horseflies, over the skeleton of the fifteen year-old Ludmilla Felfernig, whose swollen body, mouth agape, hair soaked and clogged with sand, was pulled out of the Drava by firemen — the twelve-year-old boy, who used to visit the old man year in, year out, bringing him letters and messages — the old man told Maximilian the story with misty eyes, his dentures clacking — had cried terribly.

One hot summer day, when the brown horses painted with black bone stock stood already harnessed in front of the stable, their heads buried in a trough of oats, before the coffin was brought from the mourning house to the cemetery, the face of his grandfather's corpse, which had been left exposed though it had already begun to rot, swelled so fat that the hairs of his beard poked out like the spines of a hedgehog. The dead man, reeking of decay, oozed a cadaverous fluid that dripped out from the cracks in the black wooden box, down the catafalque draped in black crepe paper, and onto the floor of the mourning chamber. While the coffin containing the swollen body was carried out the door and heaved onto the hay cart, where the two brown horses smeared with bone stock were harnessed, shuddering, shaking their heads and stomping to drive away the flies, Ingo Kirchheimer, one of the dead man's sons, stood at the wide open window on the second floor of the house and let out a cackle over the surrounding mourners, who raised their heads, and over the black-dressed priest, who was lifting his damp gray aspergil for the final blessing. The corpse fluid had dripped onto the brown Carinthian suit of one of the pallbearers, & he vomited beside a funeral wreath propped up against a garden fence. On its black ribbon, in golden letters, was written A Last Goodbye. *Let all our thoughts be winging, to where Thou didst ascend, and let our hearts be singing: "We seek Thee, Christ, our friend, Thee, God's exalted Son, our Life, & way to Heaven."*

FROM TIME TO TIME — the ninety-year-old man with the gray-flecked moustache and the trimmed eyebrows used this turn of phrase repeatedly when speaking of his childhood and youth — his uncle Ingo Kirchheimer, who stood cackling at the second floor window of the mourning house while his father's body was carried out the door for its final blessing, so that the black-dressed priest, lifting his gaze, let the damp aspergil drop back into the dented copper vessel, would go on foot from Kindelbrücken to Pulsnitz and bang a stone against the iron rail in front of the Kirchheimer estate, presided over by his brother, until a few heads poked out over the crossbars of the parlor window. Then he would vanish without entering the house. After suffering a bullet wound in the First World War, Ingo Kirchheimer, the great-uncle of the bone collector Maximilian, was admitted to the insane asylum in Klagenfurt, & appears only to have left, save for a few minor excursions with his relatives, three decades later, in a coffin. His brother Florian used to visit him now and then in the psychiatric hospital and bring him a package of speck, sausage, and homemade bread, the scent of which he would savor for a moment. He would inhale deeply before unwrapping the crackling wax paper and withdrawing his snack. Sometimes he extended a hand in greeting to his visitors, other times no, it always depended *on what his schedule was like,* those were the old man's exact words. In a photo of his grave, long-neglected, in the Annabichler cemetery in Klagenfurt, a white marble plaque is visible — but no cross — set in an iron base engraved with his name and his birth and death dates. On All Saints' Day, before pressing the button on his camera, the photographer lit a candle on the grave, atop which stood a pot of bushy white chrysanthemums.

Maximilian's great uncle, who went insane in a trench in Yugoslavia, died in the asylum in Klagenfurt in the same year that Hildegard Zitterer, in a mourning chamber hung in black, lifted the then three-year-old Maximilian over a coffin decorated with periwinkles and showed the child the ash-gray countenance of his deceased maternal grandmother, & the same year as well in which the painter and priest Balthasar Kranabeter had a calvary that he himself had painted erected in the center of town, across from the schoolhouse. The sinner lies among the leaping flames of Hell, his hands aloft, crying out in pain. A thick green serpent winds around his naked torso, slithering up to his head. Lucifer bends over the blasphemer, his red wings like bat wings fluttering in the heat — you can count their veins

— & spills a cup full of gall into his mouth. *Toi qui sais tout, grand roi des choses souterraines, Guérisseur familier des angoisses humaines, Ô Satan, prends pitié de ma longue misère!* During the consecration of the calvary, the pastor, pointing out the features of the afflicted, recollected to the faithful, holding their candles, the man who threw a statue of Jesus as large as a grown man down over a stone in a stream bed and, in recompense for his blasphemy, was crippled in the Second World War. A hand grenade tore both his arms from his body in a trench. Balthasar Kranabeter recalled that he had salvaged the life-sized Jesus with the broken arms from the stream bed with his own two hands, and had carried it though cliff and valley, over meadows & forest paths, into the village, this our village, built in the form of a cross! In the clay vessel in which the pandapigl was rendered from the bones of slaughtered animals, to mask the horse's skulls and protect them from the horseflies and mosquitoes, lies the skeleton of Ingo Kirchheimer, who was laid in his coffin in the asylum by two men in green coats with moustaches, crosswise over the bones of his father, dead in the hot summer, his corpse swollen & secreting fluid.

ALSO THE FETID CORPSE of the obese Christian Lichtegger — his skeleton lies in the clay vessel where the putrid-smelling stock was rendered from the bones of slaughtered animals, to be brushed on the horses with a crow's feather, around the eyes and nostrils and on the belly, to protect them from the mosquitoes and horseflies, over the skeleton of Ingo Kirchheimer, who lost his mind and died in an insane asylum — swelled up with gases as he lay exposed in his home in the summer heat. The wood of the narrow coffin began to creak and pop as the frightened mourners, seated around the open coffin for nocturnes clicking their beads, cried out in sorrow and prayed their rosaries.

AT THE RÖTHMEYERS', the ninety-year-old man with the gray-flecked moustache and the trimmed eyebrows recollected, there lived a Miss Dörflinger, an alleged sorceress who stayed in a room bare of furniture with the exception of four or five beds. Whenever the ten-year-old boy would visit his schoolmates, the children would crack the bedroom door and slam it back shut, and the unhinged woman, with whom it was impossible to speak, would be crouched, her hands tied, in one of the beds. When she was almost ninety and — as the ninety-year-old man said — refused to die, she spent weeks lamenting, and shouted in pain, and it was only when she was taken from the house that her plaints came to an end and she perished in the open air, in accordance with her wishes. *Especially in my final need, when others have abandoned me, when death startles and Hell threatens, let the cross protect me!*

The skeleton of Miss Dörflinger, who perished in the open air under the rain and hail without a word of complaint, pelted by hailstones that lodged in the folds of her grave clothes and in her hair, lies in the clay vessel where the bone stock was rendered from the bones of animals, to be brushed on the horses with a crow's feather around the eyes and nostrils and on the belly, to protect them from the mosquitoes & horseflies, over the skeleton of Christian Lichtegger, whose obese cadaver, reeking of decay, swelled so dreadfully that the praying mourners, who were given a few packets of coffee and sugar for their amicable services, paused in horror, holding handkerchiefs to their noses, when they heard the coffin creak.

THE NINETY-YEAR-OLD MAN with the gray-flecked moustache and the trimmed eyebrows, his hands chapped, cracked and swollen, spoke again of his childhood, leafing through a photo album, and said that, when he was not yet twelve years old, he fell four meters with a straw bale in his hands from the hayloft to the threshing floor and was knocked unconscious. My God, the boy! his father cried & dragged him unconscious from the barn into the farmhouse, where they sprinkled spring well water on his neck, and he was awakened by his parents' loud praying. Two hours later, said the old man, smiling, I was back in the hayloft with a bale of straw in my hands. Luckily my head landed in the straw pile, otherwise I would have broken my neck on the hard floor.

On the outskirts of town lived Georg Fuhrmann, who used to relieve himself in the town square in Spittal-on-the-Drava. After slaughtering the pigs on his farm, he would piss into the sausage meat, and, instead of marinating it in garlic stock, he and his wife would knead the urine soaked pork and stuff it in the pale gray, flushed and cleaned intestines. At that time, when I was twelve, the old storyteller recalled, Fuhrmann tried to shove me face-first into his excrement. While I clung to his pants legs screaming, he forced my head down, pressing on my neck, a few centimeters over the still fuming pile. But when my father came across my tormentor a few days later, Fuhrmann shouted from a distance: Please, Kirchheimer, don't kill me!

In late spring, from his fourteenth year on, he and his older brother Lazarus would drive their more than thirty sheep from his parents' farm in Pulsnitz to the alpine pastures of Rosanie in Innerkrems, some forty kilometers away, where he had lived with his asthmatic grandmother for two summers when he was five and six in a small cabin built overlooking a brook; he used to hear the murmur of the water day and night, the chirping of crickets throughout the day, and in the evening, the croaking of frogs. Not seldom, he said, a frog or toad would hop under the dining table and land on his naked toes. Once or twice each summer the young man would take his bicycle to Innerkrems, go up to Rosanie, & count the sheep, bringing them grain and a few kilos of pink salt. On the way back, to protect his rims and brake pads going downhill, he would cut down a bushy spruce from the forest's edge and tie it to the basket with the branches facing outward, so that, when he coasted downhill, they would open up and slow him down. Arriving in the valley, he would throw the dusty remains of the spruce with its broken twigs into the stream, and continue down the narrow street through the valley, following the banks of the Lieser to his home.

Four months later, in September, usually a few days before the Pulsnitz town fair, he would go on foot to Innerkrems with his older brother Lazarus, the one with the thick earlobes, accompanied by a dog, and the next morning, as soon as it was light out, they would look for the sheep. Among the thousands of sheep that grazed throughout the summer on the plain, which many farm people came from afar to use, the brothers searched out their own. Staring out from the kitchen window, his eyelids narrowed, the red & yellow autumn leaves falling from a maple tree, Maximilian's father remembered, smiling proudly: I recognized the sheep by their faces! Most of the time we made it back to Pulsnitz with the flock for the evening prayers. One time, he said, when we were already surely twenty-five, Schaflechner & I stole two sheep from another farmer as we were leaving the meadow and we sold them on our way back. That's how we made our money for the fair!

During the First World War, when the bakery closed down in Kindelbrücken, the bone collector's grandfather, Florian Kirchheimer, bought the baker's carriage with its a row of small windows down the side and its double-wing door in the rear. He went from farmhouse to farmhouse in the carriage to load up the full milk cans and drive them to the station in Kindelbrücken. The milk cans were lifted onto a train car, unloaded in Villach, and delivered to the dairy. He used to harness a half-blind nag to the carriage — a veteran from Russia, they called it — it kicked so violently that when he went to the stable to brush it, he would bend one leg back and slide a steel hoop over it to keep from getting struck. After brushing him, the horse-breeder, Maximilian's grandfather, would piss into his hand & shine the animal's head and flanks with his urine.

As a fourteen-year-old, Maximilian's father, now a ninety-year-old man with a gray-flecked moustache and trimmed eyebrows, would go day after day, in summer and in winter, from farm to farm in the surrounding villages, collecting the full milk cans and bringing them to the station. In the wintertime, sitting in the baker's carriage, he would wrap his lower body in a wool blanket. When it was especially cold, he would run, the reins in his hand, beside the vehicle with the one-eyed nag. One day, when he had missed the early train and had to wait with the milk cans for the next one, the village barber, who used to always wear a shirt with a tall, rigid white collar — a firebreak, people called it — showed up late as well. Holding his top hat fast to his head, the barber ran alongside the departing train, beckoning it to stop, but in those days, starting the train was what used up the most energy, it was said to cost twenty schillings. Once the baker's carriage and the black, one-eyed nag tied to it were chased through the town by a pack of bellowing dogs led by a big white one, which the fourteen-year-old used to rile up every day when he passed it, kicking his feet against the floorboard of the carriage, until the townspeople, the barber, the butcher, the tanner and the tailor burst out of their shop doors, their tools in their hands.

Another time, when he had already hauled the full milk cans onto the train car and come back with the one-eyed nag, its face black with the bone stock that warded off the stinging and blood-sucking horseflies and mosquitoes, the boy, then seventeen, was told by his aunt, who had stopped the carriage, that his uncle Leopold Höfferer had died of tuberculosis & was lying exposed in his house in Kindelbrücken. The young man jumped from the baker's carriage, tied the reins of the one-eyed nag to an iron ring beside the linden tree, and crossed the street to the house of mourning. In the dead man's room, he stood before his uncle, who still lay in bed, though already in a black suit, his hands folded over his breast, and his aunt whispered: Boy, make the sign of the cross over your forehead! And, with his right thumb still reeking of milk, he traced a cross over his forehead, lips, and breast, prayed an Our Father, took the spruce twig from the coffee mug filled with holy water and flung the drops that clung to the needles over the deceased. The drops sat a long time on the yellow skin of the dead man's face, but they soaked immediately into the cotton of his black suit.

In the summertime, after delivering the milk cans to the station, he would loose the one-eyed nag from the baker's carriage, hitch it to a single-bladed plow, and help his uncle till his fields. His four cousins, his uncle's daughters, in white, arm-length gloves, would plant potatoes in the furrows, chanting hymns and traditional songs, the old man of ninety with the gray-flecked moustache and the trimmed eyebrows said.

Just after the Great War, Florian Kirchheimer commissioned at his own expense the first — completely unprofitable — power plant in Pulsnitz, with money which, as his now ninety-year-old son still complains, could have paid for all the lowlands in Pulsnitz, or else for a farmhouse with fields and woods. When the first electric light was installed in the church, which was previously lit with wax candles, a worker on his lunch break left a scrap of speck in the mouth of a statue of Saint Peter. Around the head of the Virgin Mary, standing in the middle of the altar, was placed a crown of light bulbs, lit up for the first time for the blessing of the tombs on All Saints' Day in 1918. The townspeople paid for their electricity according to the quantity of bulbs, but almost none of them had money when I went into town to collect from them, Maximilian's father said. The parish house got a bulb free, because a part of the retaining wall for the power plant had to be built on church property. We also gave power to the church. Nischelwitzer got six free bulbs as well, because we built a tool shed on his land. There were two electric engines in the village in those days, and the farmers used to lend them to one another to hook up the feed cutter and the grain miller. The days each person could plug in an electric motor were strictly determined, because the power would give out if both were running in the village at the same time. It was strictly forbidden for the townspeople to plug in an electric iron, one iron used up so much power that the lights in the other houses would start to flicker. When the lights began again to blink and go dim, I knew who had plugged in the iron. I went to the Schaflechners', opened the kitchen door, pointed at the woman with her wrinkled clothes, and said: Mrs. Lenhart, who gave you permission to plug in that iron? If you plug the iron in again, I'll shut off your power!

In wintertime, when little water flowed through the village stream, I used to go at ten at night along the frozen banks with an oil lamp, through the gulley into the pitch-black forest, to close off the drain to the reservoir, which measured thirty meters long and six meters wide, and let it replenish. It would fill up to a depth of four meters. If I had slipped on the ice with that oil lamp & fallen in, I would surely have lost my life, to this day I can't swim. At five in the morning, when it was still dark, I would go with the oil lamp over the stream banks, often in thigh-deep snow, climb up the black gully, moss-covered & hung all over with icicles, into the forest, to let the dammed-up water flow into the pipes so the power plant could start up. Then the light bulbs would begin again to glow, in the church, the houses, & the stables.

Once, Maximilian's father said, the water conduit froze up. It was eighty meters in length, & ran from the reservoir to the shack where the turbine, the diameter of which — he pointed to the clock on the kitchen wall — was as big as a clock face, was hooked up to a motor. The pipes of the water conduit were full of ice. They were all Mannesmann pipes, 150's, he emphasized. Me, my father Florian, and the farmhand hung a cauldron full of hot coals from the pipe and heated it up until the ice inside began to melt, we slid it, bit by bit, down the pipe, until we'd made it to the reservoir, and the ice had melted & the power plant was back to work. It took three days to heat up the pipe, there was an eighty meter long bar of ice inside, as thick as a man's thigh. We burned through almost a whole shed full of wood!

DURING ADVENT, when the kitchen smelled of fresh-baked gingerbread, and his sister would brush egg white onto the gingerbread dough, cut into hearts, stars, and half-moons, before putting the next tray into the oven, the bone collector asked his ninety-year-old father whether his parents had given him presents, and if so, what kind, in his childhood. The ninety-year-old wrinkled his forehead, arched his trimmed eyebrows, laid his worn, heavy hands one atop the other, their nails trimmed irregularly and chipped in places, and said that on his twentieth birthday — he was born on Christmas Eve — there lay a pair of leather gaiters under the Christmas tree. In wintertime, before he went out in the loaded horse-sleigh to spread manure over the fields with a pitchfork, he would tie them around his calves to keep out the snow. At twilight, when he was done manuring the fields and had come home in the horse sleigh and led the sweating horse to the watering trough, the gaiters would be frozen stiff, with ice around the edges. From his laces, glazed with ice, sharp little icicles hung down over his leather shoes, snapping off when he'd take the restless horse from the trough through the door of the stable. The horse would chomp at its bit, leaking cold well water & foamy spit that dripped down into the snow.

When he was twenty — he recalled in laughter, breaking open a still-warm gingerbread star — he had taken a scrap of speck without asking permission from a cupboard that still stands in the attic, its door-flaps inset with two porous metal plates the size of kitchen clocks, and gone with it into the servants' quarters. Afraid of his father Florian, he had hidden under the bed with a knife, a slice of bread, & the speck, and begun to eat. Shortly afterward the farmer entered the room, looking for his son, saw the hobnailed Goiserer shoes sticking out from under the bed, the gray wool socks folded over their uppers, & shouted: Boy, what are you doing under the bed? Embarrassed, the twenty-year-old crawled out from under the pallet stuffed with cornhusks and said, red-faced, with his mouth full: Father! I took a piece of speck without asking. — That's no reason for you to hide. Eat when you like! In those days, said the ninety-year-old man, chewing warm gingerbread, I was so hungry, I'd gladly have eaten the devil's ears.

A FEW DECADES LATER, on a cold and windy spring day, his ninety-year-old father Florian, who suffered from cancer of the gall bladder & who also wore a gray-flecked moustache, was in the woodshed helping him sharpen the stakes they used to fence off their fields. He caught a cold, stayed sick throughout the summer, and even in early autumn had not gotten better. One

September morning, before his fifty-seven-year-old son, then a father five times over & inheritor of the estate, had hitched the black horse to the cart loaded with grain to take it to Fox Meadow to sow the winter rye, he visited his father, who moreover was suffering from gout, to ask him how he was. The ninety-year-old, lying in bed, whispered falteringly: Don't skimp on the harvesting, there's always more & more people eating bread! At night, after working in the stable, when he went back into his parents' room and his mother, seated on the green divan whispering her rosary, glanced up into the old mirror that hung on the wall between the two windows, bearing a warped reflection of her husband's white-haired head staring out over the sheets, the dying man asked after his youngest grandson: Where is Reinhard? But the six-year-old was already asleep and would not be roused. Moments later Maximilian's grandfather, his eyes wide open, began to gasp and rattle violently. With a handkerchief, his son cleaned the mucus that dripped in ever-greater quantities from his moustache and chin. After a few minutes' death struggle — he kept striking the coverlet with his right hand — his head sank to one side. His son made the sign of the cross over his forehead with his right thumb and closed his eyes. The next morning, the children were given used wax candles, their wicks already black, which were lit out in the corridor. They walked single-file into the mourning chamber, lined up before the deathbed, & recited in tears Our Father who art in heaven, hallowed be thy name, thy kingdom come. The fingers of the dead man who lay on the bed, already dressed in his best suit, were wound with a rosary, and a small silver crucifix had been wedged between the palms of his hands. Elisabeth, the fat, toothless grandmother, lay praying & whimpering in her marital bed, clutching a black rosary at the dead man's side. Three or four wax candles, flickering restlessly and softly crackling in the wind, were warped in the gold-framed mirror.

Three days & three nights Maximilian's grandfather lay exposed in the farmhouse, which was draped in black. On the first, or perhaps it was the second day, Maximilian's oldest brother saw that the dead man's mouth had opened slightly. He went to his mother in the kitchen and told her what he had seen, hoping his grandfather, in a few minutes or hours, would stand up and emerge from his coffin: Mama, Grandpa opened his mouth! Yeah, sure! replied his mother, dressed in black, indifferently, splitting onions and preparing a big pot of goulash. From the village and outskirts people came with coffee and sugar, offered their condolences to the slack-jawed, toothless woman, sitting black-clothed and fat in her gray felt slippers before the coffin, then took a seat and prayed for a while until they were called into the kitchen by the dead man's hunchbacked daughter Hildegard and served a plate of goulash and a roll. One person drank a beer, the rest spring water, rosehip tea was brewed, & a bottle of homemade schnapps stood on the table.

The blue and white packets of Linde coffee, the black & yellow tins of Melanda coffee, and the brown packs of rock sugar were placed by Maximilian, eight years old at the time, in a chest that also contained a well-handled book on human health. Leafing through this book when he knew his mother was away — she was often to be found, above all on the hot summer days, in the cemetery, watering the graves of her mother and her three brothers fallen in the war — he would consider the sex organs of the men and women, stare at the colored viscera and the skeleton, and trace the red blood vessels with his index finger. At the next village fair, he bought a small white plastic skeleton, which lay for months under the lamp on his night table, next to his Karl May books, and sometimes his mother or sister, cleaning the child's room, would take it aside and wipe the dust from it. No one dared to throw the plastic skeleton with the red eyes in the trash or on the cemetery waste heap. A few hours before the burial, Maximilian's father went with the five children to the garden and cut down the large, varicolored gladiolas. Kids! Take a few more flowers to grandpa! One of them lifted the pall and the others laid gladiolas over the legs of the dead man, who was covered all over with flowers from the garden. Beside his sunken cheeks lay the blossoms of two rust-red gladiolas.

It was a beautiful fall day when Florian Kirchheimer, the patriarch, was laid in his grave, no rain, no thunder, no hailstones beat down on the open black umbrellas or drummed against the coffin's black lid with its nailed-on crucifix, nor did they lodge in the cuffs on the men's trousers. The wife of the deceased, Maximilian's decrepit grandmother, fat & toothless in her black mourning clothes, did not accompany her husband to his final resting place. She stayed seated in the mourning house, squeezing the black cartilage of the rosary and praying in an arm chair in the empty mourning chamber, while the funeral director Sonnberger and a young assistant disassembled the catafalque, took the black shrouds printed with silver crosses off of their wood frames, and placed the four long electric candlesticks in the black hearse with the milk glass windows. Peeking through the broad, transparent beams of the crosses etched into the milk glass windowpanes, one might see the funerary utensils in the carriage's interior, or even a coffin overlaid with flowers. The toothless widow, dressed in black, who had stayed in the empty death chamber, could not see the peacock, just beside the calvary, its wheel of feathers unfurled, as the funeral train approached the open gates of the graveyard, led by the sacristan carrying a cross, the black-clothed priest, and the acolytes with the censer and aspergil. Nor the peahen, rooting for grain behind the calvary, which took flight with a cry that echoed through the village after the coffin had been carried past the howling sinner reclining among the towering flames on the floor of Hell, a serpent wound around his naked torso while red-winged Lucifer bent over him, before lighting on the ridge of a roof where the two birds often passed the night, huddled down after the call for prayers; but the fat, black-clothed widow, praying her rosary in the empty death chamber, had heard the bird's cry, off in the distance but rather clear, & it disturbed the rhythm of her prayers for a moment, so that she went back to the beginning of the phrase she had just begun. In the cleared-out mourning chamber nothing remained on the night table but the coffee cup, now nearly empty of holy water, with the spruce twig still inside. Beneath the window, and scattered through the room, were trampled rosebuds, carnations, and gladiolas. Candlewax, spilled out or overflowing, had hardened into star-shapes and clung to the wood floor. Tomorrow morning or the day after, they will scrape it off with a kitchen knife & sweep it up with the leftover flowers strewn about, then there will be no more traces of a dead man in the house, the mourning house will smell no more of rotten flowers, burnt spruce twigs, and wax candles.

In the clay vessel where the pandapigl was rendered from the bones of animals, to be brushed on the horses with a crow's feather around the eyes & nostrils and on the belly, to protect them from the mosquitoes & horseflies, Florian Kirchheimer's skeleton lies over the bones of

Leopold Höfferer, dead from tuberculosis. They wiped away the blood-smeared bits of straw that clung to his face and hair before they carried his corpse from the stables to the house. *Worship, for to be here is our highest reward. Give us not only thy blessing, O Lord, but thy flesh & blood divine; all that we have, in recompense, our hearts, our souls, are thine.*

WITH RED EYELIDS AND TEAR-GLAZED EYES, the farmer with the gray-flecked moustache and the trimmed eyebrows walked in through the kitchen door, threw his arms open in horror & cried: Aunt Waltraud is dead! She collapsed behind the counter of the pastry shop. A heart attack! The fat Aunt Waltraud, master baker and proprietress of the Rabitsch pastry shop in the Lindwurmplatz in Klagenfurt, renowned throughout the land, died two days before Christmas Eve, a few days after she had sent the sweets for the Christmas tree to her nieces and nephews in the village sixty kilometers away. While the children decorated the Christmas tree, pulling angel's hair, tinsel strips, chocolate horseshoes, chocolate half-moons, chocolate pinecones filled with walnut cream, chocolate butterflies, candles and frogs & jam-filled bonbons wrapped in colored crepe paper from the bed of wood shavings on the bottom of the Rabitsch pastry shop box, hanging them on the Christmas tree with copper hooks and setting the colored candles in their little holders, their grandmother Elisabeth, fat and toothless, moaned & wheezed, praying her rosary in bed, lifting her head now and then to stare at the shimmering angel's head framed in a golden star crowning the freshly cut spruce tree, groaning & clicking her rosary. The noise of the Christmas ornaments being hung up and arranged, the clack of the scissors dropped back on the table, & the noise of the bobbin falling to the floor and rolling under the grandmother's bed, mixed with the whining of the children, each ashamed before the others, crying softly for their departed aunt. Numerous times, the eleven-year-old Maximilian turned his back to his siblings & walked to the window to dry the tears from his eyes with the dirty sleeve of his shirt. While they were decorating the tree, his sister told her brothers that she had gone out to the woodshed to call their farmhand, who was chopping wood, in to eat. What's there to eat? he asked. Whatever's on the table is what there is to eat! she answered. And then the enraged servant threw his hatchet after the fleeing girl with her long braids. The hatchet slid several meters in the snow and landed near her feet.

Before the presents, Maximilian and his brother Reinhard would bathe together in the smoke kitchen in a wood tub held together by iron rings. Cursing when one of them had peed in the bathwater, they would lather themselves with a bar of turpentine soap with a stag stamped on its surface, dry their lean white bodies, the genitals still hairless, with a coarse towel beside the glowing red griddle of the wood-burning stove, and put on clean underwear, ironed shirts, and gray wool socks. While they waited on their siblings, who were taking their own bath in the smoke kitchen, where the milking machine parts were washed out & hung on hooks and where they kept the slop buckets for the hogs, they spit, out of boredom, onto the hot griddle. The drops of spittle turned spherical in the heat, dancing, hissing, brown around the edges, drawing together as they spun into the abyss, then dropped, sizzling, into the grooves of the hot griddle and evaporated among the embers. In the kitchen, it smelled of children's burnt saliva.

After a fight one summer day, under the branches of the pear tree, when Maximilian tried to spit in his cousin Egon's face, and his cousin jumped to the side at the last minute and Maximilian spit into the thin air, Egon cried: Now you've spit on the Lord God! You'll die soon, because you've spit on the Lord God! Wasps hummed around. It smelled of the reddish yellow pears that lay spongy and rotting around the tree trunk. Maximilian picked up a soft pear with the wasps clinging to its surface, sucking the sweet fruit's juice, and threw it at his cousin, who ran away, and cried: I didn't spit on our Lord God! I didn't spit on him at all! I won't die as soon as you think! Only a few months before, after the thaw, rummaging around in the cemetery waste heap behind the church, they had taken pink & yellow plastic roses and carnations from the rotten funeral wreaths and pinned them to their clothes. They used to stand on the roadside a few meters apart holding bouquets of snowdrops, waving down the cars with German license plates. The drivers would stop and buy the snowdrops. They would jump from one clump of grass to the other, picking the snowdrops in the damp forest. They never returned to the roadside after one driver stopped, took the snowdrops from their hands, and went on his way without paying.

After the siblings, the maid, the farmhand, & their parents had bathed themselves with turpentine soap in the wooden tub, washing off the odor of the stable — the stag stamped in the top of the shrunken soap had vanished entirely, his antlers and his skeleton floated off in the filthy bathwater — they walked, one after the other, from the warm kitchen through the frigid corridor of the stone house, past the smoke kitchen, up the sixteen steps of the staircase into their grandparents' bedroom, whence their dead grandfather Florian had recently been carried off and where their grandmother Elisabeth, her toothless mouth open, laid out in bed gasping desperately, lifted her head, covered in sparse white hair, from the hollow in her pillow, which smelled of unwashed scalp, sebum, and dried spit, on seeing her grandchildren enter. Maximilian's sister, holding in her lap her five-month-old brother, who stared at the glittering tinsel of the Christmas tree, had taken her grandmother's customary seat, between her father and mother, on the sunken-in divan reeking of urine. Maximilian and his brother stood just beside the Christmas tree, the deaf maid and the stuttering farmhand behind them. After lighting the colored Christmas tree candles and the sparklers that hung in every corner the tree, throwing sparks over the branches and down onto the presents and deepening the pervading scent of spruce, they began to pray for their dead grandfather, and for their mother's three brothers who had fallen in the war, and tears drained from their eyes and snot from their noses, until their father, who led the prayers, began an Our Father and a Hail Mary for Aunt Waltraud, who had died two days before, still lay exposed in the Annabichler funeral home in Klagenfurt, and would not be buried until after Christmas. While the father, a little shortsighted, raised his trimmed eyebrows & wrinkled his forehead to read the nametags and pass out the presents, the children continued mourning Aunt Waltraud — she had come to visit one summer day, when their grandfather was still alive, & had brought the children their first ice creams, lemon and vanilla, in an insulated box from her pastry shop. Their tears, tickling their cheeks & dripping down onto the boxes, softened the wrapping paper covering a flannel shirt, a pair of wool socks, or long underwear. Each one of them could take some sweets down from the Christmas tree, the children also gave the maid and the farmhand chocolate pinecones and varicolored gelatin stars coated in sugar. Nor did Maximilian's sister neglect to give the stammering farmhand a chocolate half-moon and a pair of chocolate pliers. With their fingers, the children smoothed out the colored wrappings, printed with pinecones, chimney-sweeps, lucky clovers, rocking horses, frogs, and butterflies, and slid them as bookmarks into their storybooks and Karl May novels.

For two hours after the presents and the evening snack — sitting around the kitchen table, they ate homemade pork sausages with horseradish & mustard, which squirted grease, to the children's diversion, as far as a meter away when stuck with a fork — the mother, father, and children prayed the rosary for the dead, with the mother leading. The deaf maid, who could read lips, stayed in the kitchen and prayed along, glancing often at the mother's mouth. The farmhand, after his snack, retired into his unkempt hovel, its floor littered with straw blades and cigarettes, the soap foam dried on the shaving brush, and the stable shoes, their edges caked with excrement, lying upturned in front of the bed. He smoked a few hand-rolled cigarettes, sipped from a schnapps bottle with a gentian pictured on its label, undressed and went to sleep. The children put on their new checked flannel shirts, the stiff collars chafing their skin, and the thick long underwear the color of viscera, and went with their parents and the maid through the unlit, snow-caked village street, to the church for midnight mass. Only the Shaflechners had left their porch light on, shining down over the village street; and here and there, inside the other houses, a few lamps remained lit. Children and adults, wearing their brand-new clothes, appeared in their doorways & headed toward midnight mass, stamping through the virgin snow. Even the calvary, where the painting pastor, Balthasar Kranabeter, had depicted Hell, was unlit, covered with a cap of snow. Crab-red Lucifer, pointy-eared and hook-nosed, his red wings unfurled, thick horns growing from his forehead, and long, bloody nails sprouting from his fingers, bent over the man lying on the floor in torment, beseeching release from Father Abraham, after throwing a life-sized Christ over a cliff decades before — later to be salvaged from the stream bed with his arms snapped off by the pastor, who stood him in the entranceway to the parish house & adorned him with seasonal flowers. Around the nude torso of the profaner of Christ winds a green serpent, fat and suffocating. Lucifer spills a cup of gall into his mouth. Left and right blaze the searing flames of Hell, smelling of myrrh and incense. *Toi qui, même aux lépreux, aux parias maudits, Enseignes par l'amour le goût du Paradis, Ô Satan, prends pitié de ma longue misère!* The light from the stained glass windows in the church, already long lit up in anticipation of Christ's birth, fell on the grave of Ludmilla Felfernig, the fifteen-year-old maidservant and suicide, who smeared menstrual blood on her face and the head of the devil on her knees before the calvary, praying to her guardian angel, and then ran barefoot over the stubble field, with blood-drenched hands and thighs, and threw herself, screaming, into the Drava. In the snow hills over the grave mounds, little spruce trees had been placed, decorated with candles and tinsel.

After the midnight mass in the ice-cold church, the parish cook gave a package to the eleven-year-old Maximilian in front of the cemetery gate and said: Quick, hide it! Hide it right away! With the package under his anorak he walked by the calvary — a vase stood in front of Hell, filled with blossoming white and red Saint Barbara branches — down the snowy village street. The cotton-soft snow crunched under the soles of his shoes. Here and there he saw, on the second floors of the farmhouses, the peaks and upper branches of the decorated firs and spruces. The two peacocks were nowhere to be seen, they would already have taken shelter in the warm stable, near the cattle ramp. Snowflakes fell on the blue-green peacock-feather eyes lying on the gangway. Would the candles on the Christmas tree on grandfather's tomb already have burned out? Burnt black angels' hair in the branches of the little tree, soot-blackened silver tinsel. Snow crystals lodged in the crowns of iron thorns on the rusty crucifixes standing behind the gravestones. Two or three small green frogs, with slivers of host in the corners of their mouths, sliding repeatedly down the gold walls of the chalice, powerless to scale its rim and flee the tabernacle. Eyebrows ablaze. Even the footprints of the two peacocks were long snowed over. Ice muffled the murmur of the snow-covered village stream. Filthy beast! they said, when Maximilian trapped a crawfish after a flood & brought it to the kitchen in a washbasin to show everyone. The centimeters-high snow piled on the power lines fell to the ground like white ribbons, now from one cable and now from another. Snow dropped silently from the fir trees as well, ten, twenty meters high, standing snug at the forest's edge, and also from the slender branches of the birches. Snowflakes tickled his face and gathered in his hair, quickly melting in the part. He kicked off the centimeters-thick snow from the soles of his shoes against the house's outer wall. In the kitchen, he reached in his jacket pocket & scattered a fistful of incense he had scooped up in the sacristy — the pastor, at that moment, had been pulling his cassock over his white-haired head — over the hot griddle, where it smoked & crackled. The last snowflakes still in his hair melted in the kitchen's heat, drained into his scalp, and ran sporadically down the back of his ears and onto his neck. He untied the package the parish cook had given him at the cemetery gate, and pulled *Im Sudan* and *Durchs wilde Kurdistan* from the crinkling wrapping paper, decorated with winged angel heads, bodiless and blowing trumpets.

Where then were the angel heads, winged and disembodied, that his mother, some years back — Angel of

God, my guardian dear, to whom my heart commends me here — had threaded with fine gold chains and hung around her children's necks? Maximilian was five or six when he went out in the snow during Advent, barefoot and dressed only in pajamas, hoping to meet the parish cook out walking in the village street, and his sister followed him and dragged him back to the warm kitchen. Not a week later, in keeping with the wishes of the pastor Balthasar Kranabeter, Maximilian, in his red acolyte's tunic, knelt before the altar at the priest's feet as he said mass.

Maximilian leafed through the pages of the books, sniffed inside them, read the tables of contents of the two Karl May books, which told of slave-traders and hippopotamus hunts, kept them out of the hands of his brother, who was rubbing his cold fingers together, went to the children's room, heated by a still-warm wood burning stove, and laid the books on the night table. In front of it he placed his felt slippers and crawled under the bedcover. Only a tuft of brown hair peeked out. He prayed his evening prayers before sleeping. *Before I lay me down to sleep, I pray the Lord my soul to keep. And if I die before I wake, I pray the lord my soul to take.*

Just once he would like to see nativity figures bigger than the Christmas tree behind them, it is always the Christmas tree dwarfing Mary, Joseph, and the Christ child, never those three, with the three wise men, larger than life, each with a Christmas tree lit with sparklers in hand, coming from behind the tall firs of the forest, densely snow-capped & collapsing down over us like a landslide, a torrent of mud, showering us with light and splendor, with sparklers and candlewax, wrapping us in angels' hair smelling of frankincense and myrrh, burying us beneath chocolate crucifixes and prayer books — our chocolate rocking horses — with candy rosaries, ice cubes of holy water, chocolate waning moons & rising suns; but on the table, where a tapered fir tree emerges from a wooden cross, they stand small and wretched, year after year, Mary, Joseph, and the Christ child, carved from spruce wood, their haloes overlaid with cherry veneer. Two images hang in the holy corner, one leaning in toward the other: Jesus stares from one; from the other, the mother of God looks down on the tuft of hair peeking out from under the comforter. Packets of funeral notices from the village dead gather dust behind the sacred images. Jesus shows his heart pierced by arrows, his mother Mary has a white lily in her hand. The glimmering silver peak of the Christmas tree, reflecting the children's room, the parents, the grandmother, the maid, & the farmhand, turns toward Jesus' arrow-pierced heart, which will bleed and bleed, & then shall the blood of Christ be shed over the shimmering Christmas tree, down over the branches, snuffing the candles & sparklers, sweeping away the wood figurines, Mary, Joseph, & the Christ child. Go with thy family into the ark! Take the beasts of the earth as well!

In the clay vessel where the putrid-smelling bone stock was rendered from the bones of slaughtered animals, to be painted on the horses with a crow's feather around the eyes and nostrils and on the belly, to protect them from the mosquitoes & horseflies, lies the skeleton of Aunt Waltraud, who collapsed before her customers in the Rabitsch pastry shop in Klagenfurt in the middle of wrapping up a sponge cake, over the bones of Florian Kirchheimer, Maximilian's grandfather, who died at ninety in his farmhouse of cancer of the gall bladder and who for a time, only a few years before his death, used to dress his two grandchildren, who were not yet old enough for school, until Maximilian began screaming in the mornings, refusing to be touched by the tall surly gentleman who wheezed audibly through his humid gray-flecked moustache and who, when he buttoned the boy's shirt, would always graze his grandson's chest with his yellow fingers, cold, bony and shivering. Maximilian would hide from his screaming grandfather — Come here, come here, you're going to mind me! — and wait for his mother, who was in the stable feeding hot potatoes to the pigs. Her black hair always smelled of the cows she had just come from milking. Seated on the milking stool, she used to press her head into the brown and white flanks of the milk cow. Scraps of boiled potatoes clung to her apron. Her fingertips, too, were cold, sliding the buttons through the eyelets. Child! she would say, why won't you let grandpa dress you? He's not going to do anything!

Thou shalt in majesty return when the world has met its grave, then shall I face Thee, O mighty God, your weak & trembling slave. O say to me then, I know thee well, thou knelt at my manger and prayed.

THE HUNCHBACK HILDEGARD laid her warm, arthritis-wracked right hand over the cold hands of her husband, wound through with a rosary and folded in prayer, shook his corpse until the coffin began to rock from the black-draped catafalque, and wailed: Willi! Willi! Willibald, who had worked for decades in the Heraklith factory on the other bank of the Drava, was dead from lung cancer. His hands in the air and his pants around his ankles, he stepped out of the bathroom and called: Hilde! Hilde! Help me! then fell over & died on the spot. After working in the factory, he was often to be met with smoking a pipe in the garden, where, alongside a row of red, black, & white currants, he had also planted gooseberries and flowers. Grass snakes, slithering over from the nearby swamp, would sun themselves on the hot glass of the lettuce cloches and had to be driven away with a hazelnut switch so that Helene & her sister Hildegard could lift open the glass panels in the afternoon & cut a few heads of lettuce. It always used to scare me, Helene would say, when I had to chase away the snakes, often they would wrap themselves around the stick. Sometimes she had found snakeskins among the broad green leaves of the lettuce heads she had cut. Then I would lose my appetite, said black-haired Helene with a grimace. After playing football with his cousin Egon, and punting the leather ball through the door of the woodshed, Maximilian would sit a long time in front of the bushes that bordered the garden, picking the blue or whitish-yellow gooseberries, one after the other, squeezing them against his palate with his tongue until they exploded, then spitting the skin, thick and slightly bitter, into the grass, and swallowing the thick pulp, warmed by the sun, while Willi smoked his pipe beneath the vines in the garden. A white mutt — Pomeranian and Dachshund — which answered to the name of Prinzi, knelt at his feet.

Helene is married to a man who even today venerates Hitler and who gets together with two other old men in the kitchen of the farm house to exchange war stories every year for All Saints' Day after the blessing of the tombs, and who, by way of punishment, used to make his daughter Karin — not yet twenty — go alone to the cesspit with a long-handled ladle to gather feces and throw them into the manure tanker with a rusty bucket, until bloody blisters formed on her hands. When his children saw their father step out of his company car at night, returning from his work as a carpenter, & walk down the hill to the house, they would run from the kitchen to the house of their aunt Hildegard and uncle Willibald, where they would hole up under the holy corner until bedtime, nibbling homemade cookies. One day, he chopped up a leather ball his two sons used to play soccer with, especially on Sundays, behind the house. When his older son had crossed the road incautiously and nearly caused a traffic accident, he ran and hid himself in Maximilian's father's barn, & when the carpenter found him, he beat him until he was half-dead.

A few years after her husband's death, Hildegard began to languish and neglect herself, she stopped washing and doing her hair, she repeated the same questions, and never remembered whether she had already eaten lunch or whether dinnertime was at hand. Hildegard, remember, took the then three-year-old Maximilian, lifted him in the air, and showed him the corpse of Leopoldine Felsberger, his maternal grandmother, who lay in a coffin covered with periwinkles, having died of heartbreak more than a decade after her three sons, all of them in the full flower of youth, fell in the Second World War. On the lower half of the coffin was draped a translucent shroud of black nylon. Her face was gray and ashy, her eyes deeply sunken. Back to this moment, Maximilian can remember, it is here that the flood of recollected images begins. Shortly before her death, when Maximilian was seventeen and his aunt Hildegard had long ceased to notice the feces and urine that streamed down her legs, over the nylon leggings held to her desiccated calves with an elastic band, she asked him whether he would, *when the time came,* follow behind her coffin. When the time did come, the relatives, especially her sister Helene, who had cared for her selflessly, were glad for an end to her sufferings, and happy that Hildegard, who spoke derangedly and always smelled of excrement, had died in the hospital in Villach, and that her brother, the now ninety-year-old man with the gray-flecked moustache and trimmed eyebrows, had taken care that she did not lie three days exposed in her bedroom, as was the custom, because she had, to use his own words, looked *off* when she was shown to him in a refrigerated chamber in the Villach hospital. A twisted countenance overcame her in death. Her cheeks and mouth were deeply sunken. *Livor mortis* dotted her face and hands. Moreover, the process of decomposition was so advanced, it was impossible to expect that the funeral guests remain seated, praying their rosary before her open coffin. Her room, where her husband Willibald had also lain exposed — during their lifetime, they were only granted a large kitchen and a bedroom in Helene's house — was again cleaned out and decorated as a mourning chamber by the funeral director Sonnberger, and her sealed coffin, surrounded by wreaths and bouquets of flowers, was stood on a catafalque draped in black. At the foot of the coffin was a small table where the death notice lay, behind a silver crucifix flanked by two burning candles, recounting that our dearly beloved Hildegard, respected by all, always ready to lend a hand, sister, sister-in-law, and aunt, had been called to eternity by our Lord,

& that we would accompany our dear deceased to her final resting place in the cemetery in Pulsnitz. Placed in front of the crucifix in a small teacup, full of the holy water her nephew had fetched from the parish house, stood a spruce twig. The attendees, come to express their condolences, crossed the threshold of the room, turned to the coffin, made the sign of the cross, said a prayer softly, took the damp twig from the teacup and sprinkled holy water on the sealed coffin, then crossed themselves again and sat in the creaky wooden chairs, closing their hands in prayer. Still today, nearly thirty years later, Maximilian hears the splash of the holy water against the coffin and the black ribbons of the wreaths. When her husband, Willibald, lay exposed — the coffin lid was propped against the bedroom wall, behind the black decorations — holy water was splashed over his corpse, which was covered by a nylon shroud, black & translucent. The drops of holy water clung to the fine weave of the shroud and ran slowly over the dark suit of the deceased, dripped into his half-open mouth and over his thick & slightly disordered moustache, stained brown from pipe tobacco. The silver crucifix between two burning candles at the dead man's feet, behind the holy water dish with the twig of spruce, was a part of the funeral director's ensemble, & after the burial, he put it back in the black Mercedes he used to drive from one mourning chamber to another throughout the Drava valley.

In late autumn and winter, especially around Christmastime, Maximilian would bring fresh milk, often still warm from the cow's body, to his uncle Willibald and aunt Hildegard. Not far from the forest's edge, he would go through the snow-covered fields with the full milk jug to the childless couple. In a single movement, the hunchbacked Hildegard would dump the milk from the brown enameled jug into a white pitcher. Without rinsing the empty jug, she would fill it half-full with home-baked macaroons, vanilla crescents, linzers, and glazed gingerbread cookies topped with colored sugar sprinkles. Returning home with the milk jug through the fields covered in hard snow — his shoes often broke through the crust, and he would sink knee-deep in the powdery snow — Maximilian would eat a few cookies softened by the last traces of milk. At home he would pass the milk jug to his mother with the rest of the soggy pastries, warm his naked feet, frozen and throbbing — his toes were all pins & needles — against the wood-burning stove, and sip the hot rosehip tea his mother had made him.

Hildegard was known and esteemed throughout the village for her exquisite sweets — Hilde, the dear soul — and her culinary endowments were gladly put to use by the townspeople & especially by her relatives, for baptisms, obsequies, weddings and fairs. When she cooked, she always wore a black velvet apron, and over it a white one, spotless & recently ironed. When her work in the kitchen was done, she would put the white apron aside and sit down at the table in the black velvet one, among her relatives, who drank coffee and ate cakes, usually beside her nieces & nephews. One time, in her sister Helene's kitchen, she took Maximilian under her protection, resting her fingers, slightly twisted from arthritis, over his brown hair & pulling his head into her breast when Uncle Friedhelm — one of the war correspondents on All Saints' Day, after the blessing of the tombs — who even to this day is proud to have been in the SS, threatened to *clip* Maximilian, to cut off his genitals. Everyone laughed as Uncle Friedhelm leapt to his feet from behind the table, still littered with cake crusts, & dug in his pants for a pocketknife. Crying, Maximilian hugged his aunt Hildegard's thigh and pressed his face into her black velvet apron with its scent of pastry. She stroked his hair & whispered over and over into his ear: Don't be afraid, I've got you! Maximilian also went with Aunt Hildegard to Villach for the first time, to have a blood analysis done. His relatives and acquaintances were struck by his alarming pallor, as they referred to it. Maximilian pulled back his arm in fear when the nurse, without warning, pricked the tip of his index finger & began drawing blood from it with a glass tube. When they went to a pharmacy after getting the results, to pick up the iron pills the doctor had prescribed, Maximilian rested his chin on the counter & smiled, and the pharmacist, seeing his rotten teeth, gave him a tube of toothpaste. Say thank you! Aunt Hildegard said to Maximilian.

From his first to his fourteenth year, usually in the evening on Holy Saturday, before the villagers said mass and lit a bonfire in the church field near the ossuary and his mother's second vegetable garden, in celebration of the resurrection of the Crucified, his godmother Hildegard would bring him his *godmother clothes* as an Easter present: pants and a shirt or a pair of leather shoes, or a suit smelling of the tailor's shop, which she would carry through the fields, muddy from the freshly thawed snow, to her brother's farmhouse in a wicker basket. When she wanted to give Maximilian a suit, Hildegard would take the boy, pale and anemic, with his prescription for iron pills, to the tailor in Kindelbrucken, a haggard little man who smelled of cigarettes & reams of fabric and took the measurements in his shop with a yellow plastic tape. The tailor, hunched down before the boy, squinting and puffing a cigarette, felt his thigh with his jittery hands, struck his calf with a flat sliver of pink tailor's soap impressed with a trademark, tossed the measuring tape over his shoulder, opened the scissors, tugged at the boy's fly with his bony fingers and adjusted the straight pins. Then Maximilian pulled up his shirt and let the tailor wrap the stiff yellow tape, cold & reinforced with thread, around his naked belly. Besides the suit in its wrapper, a big chocolate Easter bunny, and multicolored chocolate Easter eggs, Hildegard gave the boy, before the Feast of the Resurrection, a sugar-dusted coffee cake with a ten-schilling piece baked inside it. In the hole in the cake's center, in a nest of green paper, lay a dyed egg with a decal portraying an Easter lamb holding the banner of the resurrection. *The redeemer is risen, freed from death's bonds, who lashes for me bore. Alleluia. Death cannot sting me, the Easter lamb brings me to the empty grave of my Lord. The people are saved, Satan is chained, the stone has rolled from the door. Alleluia.*

In the clay vessel where the putrid-smelling bone stock was rendered from the bones of slaughtered animals, to be brushed on the horses with a crow's feather around the eyes & nostrils and on the belly, to protect them from the mosquitoes and horseflies, lies the skeleton of Willibald Zitterer, who ran stumbling from the bathroom with his hands raised and his pants around his ankles, then fell over and expired, his face in a pool of his own urine, over the skeleton of Aunt Waltraud, who died of a heart attack at the pastry shop in the Lindwurmplatz in Klagenfurt. As the stunned Hildegard lifted up her dead husband's torso, crying Willi! What's happening? warm urine dripped down her forearms. Aunt Waltraud's burial took place a few days after Christmas in the Annabichler cemetery in Klagenfurt. Scarcely had his father, then seventy years old, with a gray-flecked moustache and trimmed eyebrows, returned from Klagenfurt, walking through the kitchen door, when he said, taking his head over and over in his hands, that his brother Eduard was so drunk, he couldn't even make it to his wife's funeral.

Brief is the night that covers me, till the angel arrives to wake me. Then shall my savior come for me, and to his eternal kingdom take me. Alleluia. I shall stand before thee for my heavenly trial, and the holy lamb shall walk down the aisle. Alleluia.

In the clay vessel where the pandapigl was rendered from the bones of slaughtered animals, to be brushed on the horses with a crow's feather, around the eyes and nostrils and on the belly, to protect them from the mosquitoes and horseflies, the skeleton of Hildegard Zitterer lies atop that of her husband, Willibald Zitterer. In a family photo, taken on Maximilian's paternal grandparents' golden anniversary, two cakes rest on a table laid with a white tablecloth, & Hildegard wears a blouse from the tailor in Kindelbrucken who made Maximilian's suits, of the same cloth as was worn by her mother Elisabeth, the toothless, white-haired celebrant. The cakes in the photos — one was baked by Hildegard, Aunt Waltraud had brought the other from her pastry shop in Klagenfurt — were not yet cut. The room smelled of fresh-picked mayflowers, standing in a vase between the cakes, and of almonds — the roses and other ornaments on the cakes were made of marzipan — of spilled red wine, and of a glowing cigar, smoked with relish by the already tipsy owner of the old Rabitsch pastry shop and chauffeur of the Bishop of Gurk.

FATHER, YOU'VE STILL GOT a parcel of forest and a few heads of cattle unaccounted for, you need to write a will! the fifty-seven-year-old farmer advised his father Florian, who was already suffering from cancer of the gall bladder when they sat beside each other on the bench between the stable and the house after their work was done. Each will get his part, & the rest stays here with the house! the ninety-year-old man replied. You can say that to me, but my brothers and sisters don't have to believe me! To his two daughters as well, black-haired Helene & humpbacked Hildegard, the old man had sworn: What I leave behind, stays with the house! He never wrote a will. After his death, estate proceedings were held in Kindelbrücken. In the courtroom, fat-lobed Lazarus turned to his sister: We've got something coming to us too, our father left behind cattle & woods! After a minute's silence, during which the siblings examined one another with curiosity, each waiting for a word from the other, the farm-owner and father of five pressed his sisters: Don't just sit there, you could get something out of this too. His brother Eduard, who owned the Rabitsch pastry shop in Klagenfurt with his wife, proposed that they let the six cows, the two horses, and the remaining woodlands be signed over to their mother Elisabeth, upon which fat-lobed Lazarus, the oldest among them, objected: Then it will all go to whoever Mother likes best! At that point, the judge turned on Lazarus: Go visit your mother every day and tickle her ribs, then maybe it will be you who comes away with everything, the woods and the livestock! The six cows, the two horses, and the woodlands were transferred to the eighty-year-old Elisabeth Kirchheimer in keeping with the court's decision. The next day, the fat-lobed Lazarus went to Pulsnitz in his Mercedes, climbed the sixteen steps of the staircase, cracked the bedroom door & called to his bedridden mother in a deep, scratchy voice before crossing over the threshold: Mother, we've taken care of everything for you! That's good! That's good of you! the bedridden old woman thanked him. The fat-lobed Lazarus was not to be seen for the next two years in his mother's house, although he lived only a few kilometers' walk away.

There lived for a time in Pulsnitz a German priest, a National Socialist, who had impregnated a woman in his parish in Liesing. The woman gave birth to twins, and the priest was transferred from the Liesing parish to the Pulsnitz one, as a punishment, by the bishop. Pastor Wohlfahrt, as he was called, disappeared not long after the outbreak of the Second World War to his brother's in America, at which time it occurred to him that he should have carried his cross into the front; & when the war was over, he returned to Europe every once in a while, as a visitor. One of his brothers, a conscientious objector, was murdered by the Nazis. After Maximilian's paternal grandfather died, Pastor Wohlfahrt crossed the ocean once again and stopped in to see the fat, bedridden grandma Kirchheimer. The bedbound old woman begged him: Bring me Lazarus! After holding mass in Pulsnitz, he brought her son Lazarus back from his two-year absence. Fat-lobed Lazarus appeared in his mother's room, with his retinue and with Pastor Wohlfahrt, and sat for an hour at the sick woman's bed. But he left his parents' house without entering the kitchen or saluting his younger brother, heir to the estate, now a ninety-year-old man with a gray-flecked moustache and trimmed eyebrows.

When aunt Hildegard saw the thirteen-year-old Maximilian come in, she raised her head & squeezed a damp cloth with her left hand. Water dripped from the cloth onto the naked corpse of his grandmother Elisabeth, who lay in bed with her legs bent and spread apart. Beside the deathbed in the Biedermeyer style, a white lacquered washbasin, half-full of filthy water, sat atop a chair. From behind the curtain of gray, undulating hair falling over her face, Hildegard saw him beseeching her through eyes clouded with tears, and she lifted her chin and tilted her head toward the door. With his face turning red, he shut the door quietly, while his aunt prayed aloud, washing the corpse with a damp rag; ten years before, when he was three, she had taken his hand and walked with him through the still-unpaved village street, past the calvary, and had grasped him under the arms in the family farmhouse and lifted him up over the coffin covered in periwinkles, pulling the translucent black shroud to one side to let him see the gray, shrunken face of his maternal grandmother, Leopoldine Felsberger, who was killed, it is still rumored, decades after the fact, by an overdose injected directly into her heart. She took the boy's hand and walked back up the street toward the calvary with its image of Hell. Beneath the red flames stabbing the air, near the head of the serpent wound around the sinner's naked torso, was a vase of white and purple lilies, lush & fragrant, picked from the same garden where the daughter of the deceased had broken off from an old, knotted bush the sprigs of periwinkle they had hung on the death shroud with safety pins, poking holes through the curving green leaves. A black rooster with a blood-red comb pecked at the yellow grains of corn scattered on the floor of Hell by Oswin, the toothless, humpbacked laborer who helped the sacristan at mass. *Ô toi qui de la Mort, ta vieille et forte amante, Engendras l'Espérance, — une folle charmante! Ô Satan, prends pitié de ma longue misère!*

The body of his grandmother Elisabeth, which her daughter Hildegard had dressed after washing it, was carried off in a blanket by the funeral director Sonnberger and the then sixty-two-year-old man with the gray-flecked moustache and the trimmed eyebrows, to the bedroom where the farmhand slept, already decorated with black cloth by the funeral director. For the three days that the body lay exposed in the servant's quarters, the farmhand slept in the barn. Her son Oswald and the funeral director set the shrouded body on the floor at the threshold of the room, threw open the four corners of the blanket, grabbed the cumbersome corpse beneath the armpits and legs and laid it in the coffin, which afterward — with the help of Oswald's brother Friedhelm — they heaved onto the catafalque. The funeral director unfolded the nylon shroud with its rose petal border and draped it over the deceased. The finger bones of her folded hands, the point of her nose, her forehead, and the tips of her black-stockinged toes grazed the translucent black shroud, which hung down from the lower half of the coffin. On the black tapestry hung behind the head of the deceased, a large silver cross was printed. To the left and right of the coffin, and at the head & foot, the funeral director, smoking a cigarette, his eyes half-closed, had placed four tall electric candles, lit and crackling.

After picking up the death notices from the printer & bringing them home, the heir to the estate, who was bequeathed his dead father's eyeglasses five years before, sat at the kitchen table and began addressing them to family and acquaintances, when a white Mercedes came down the gravel driveway to the farmhouse. Without entering the kitchen — the door was cracked open — the fat-lobed Lazarus, his older brother, followed by his wife & children, walked down the narrow hallway of his parents' house to the mourning chamber and took a seat from among the row of chairs, beside the weeping women. Oswald left the pen and the glasses he had inherited from his father over the pile of black-trimmed death notices, walked from the kitchen to where his older brother sat, in front of the coffin in the mourning chamber, and offered him his hand, but the embittered Lazarus, who had hoped to take over his father's agricultural affairs and had, after his father had decided in his younger brother's favor, taken to calling the latter an *estate-robber,* avoiding all contact with him after their father's death five years back, refused his hand at first, in front of their mother, who lay exposed in the middle of the room. The younger brother aimed his index finger at the dead woman and said: So this is what we've come to! Well if you won't take my hand, so be it! Short, plump Lazarus, also with a gray-flecked moustache, stood and extended his brother his right hand. One after the other, his family followed his lead, first his wife, then his older son, and finally the youngest. Maximilian's father left the mourning chamber & walked back to the kitchen, which smelled of burnt onion and Hungarian paprika — a Szeged goulash was being prepared — & continued addressing the obituaries. Hardly half an hour had passed when, after taking the spruce twig from the foot of the coffin, lifting it forcefully over the black-stockinged feet of the deceased, & sprinkling his dead mother with holy water, Lazarus departed from the death chamber with his retinue, walked down the narrow hallway, looking neither left nor right, went without a word of greeting past the kitchen door, and sat down in the driver's seat of his white Mercedes. Each time the children visited the property while their grandfather was still alive, Lazarus' son, who had survived a grave accident as a child, would go straight into the barn, before even greeting his relatives, to scatter fodder with a pitchfork into a wooden box through a gap in the boards, and the horse, having drunk from the trough, would bury its head in the box before being led back to the stable. For three decades after his mother's death, fat-lobed Lazarus did not set foot in his parents' house nor visit his younger brother, to whom their father, after a fight with Lazarus, turned over his agricultural estate.

In the clay vessel where the putrid-smelling bone stock was rendered from the bones of slaughtered animals, to be brushed with a crow's feather on the horses, around their eyes and nostrils and on their bellies, to protect them from the mosquitoes & horseflies, Maximilian, the bone collector, shifts the skeletons of Willibald and Hildegard Zitterer, laying the skeleton of Hildegard over the bones of her mother, Elisabeth Kirchheimer, who, after long and painful suffering, a few days after she'd asked the thirteen-year-old Maximilian, who sat on the sunken-in, urine-scented sofa flipping through his Karl May book, whether he had heard the Tschufitl, the death-bird, cry out, perished in the farmhouse under the eyes of her son and the family doctor. On the branch of some spruce tree that rose up at the forest's edge, a screeching jaybird opened its wings & groomed its feathers with its beak.

The corpse of her husband, the farmer & patriarch Florian Kirchheimer, had lain exposed in the farmhouse six years before. The corpse of Elisa, his wife, who had a Slavic maiden name, was laid out in the servant's quarters half a decade later. The patriarch wore black leather shoes as he lay in the open coffin. The legs of his wife (also in an open coffin), who had cried out from fear of death at night for her son Oswald — the father of Maximilian, who spent the night, during her final days, in the same bedroom where she eventually perished — were covered only in black leggings — no shoes were put on her feet. At the deathbed of her husband, the farmer & horse-breeder, two doctors stood among the relatives, who had all been called to attend. At his wife's deathbed stood only her son Oswald & the fat, white-haired family doctor. In the wife's case, the outlay for flowers was limited as well. Maximilian's father did not order his children to go to the garden, as they had for their grandfather, to cut gladiolas, pansies, and snapdragons, and lay them over the coffin for the deceased. Pale Maximilian, with his prescription for iron pills, knew her death-throes had ended when his father and the doctor, with tears in their eyes, took leave of one another in the hallway. Mama! It's over! he said to his mother, who was standing at the stove, long tired from caring for the aggrieved. When Maximilian's brother returned home at night from his locksmith's apprenticeship, they both nodded their heads wordlessly to one another. The black-clothed pastor, painter of prayer cards and images of Hell, went weeping from the house, carrying the consecrated oil he had used in the anointing of the deceased. Maximilian's mother would often say she had felt deeply wounded when her mother-in-law purportedly said to her, a few years after the death of her own mother, who had lost three sons, in the full flower of their youth, in the Second World War: It's five years now since your mother's dropped off! She could have avoided the phrase *dropped off,* Maximilian's mother said, there were other ways she could have put it. When Hitler invaded Austria and the jeeps passed a few meters from the farmhouse over the highway running along the forest edge through the Drava valley, Elisabeth, her future mother-in-law, ran out through the door with her hands held high, crossed the yard toward the passing motorcade and cried out zealously: Heil Hitler! Heil Hitler! Just after the wedding, when Maximilian's mother left her parents' house, the Felsbergers', and moved onto the Kirchheimer estate, there wasn't even lunch on the table. She was made to kill a chicken for the family of her in-laws. Maybe, she said later, my mother-in-law Elizabeth and her jealous daughters, Hildegard & Helene, who still lived on the farm, wanted to know if I could slaughter a chicken; in any case, they watched with curiosity while I killed the animal. All three women, my mother-in-law and her two daughters, stood around me while I bent back its neck, brought the knife close, and held the wriggling, bleeding bird over the drain while it flapped its wings. I never had the feeling of being welcome in the Kirchheimer house, Maximilian's mother said. You will remember that Hildegard approached her husband's coffin, laid her arthritis-wracked fingers over her husband's cold hands, joined in prayer and woven through with a rosary, shouted Willi! Willi! disconsolately, and shook his corpse. Maximilian stood on the threshold of the mourning chamber — the door had been taken off its hinges — when his aunt Hildegard, her face contorted from sorrow, approached her mother Elisabeth, put her arthritic hands, interlaced with a rosary, over the cold hands of her mother, likewise crooked from arthritis, cried Mama! Mama! & shook her corpse. Maximilian took a step back, afraid that the black-clad body would slip from the coffin and slump down onto the floor.

It was a warm September day when the funeral train moved through the town, accompanying Elisabeth Kirchheimer, in her eighty-sixth year, on her final journey to the cemetery. Maximilian, who was not allowed to serve as acolyte that day & instead formed part of the funeral train — two other boys wore the acolytes' black uniform

— carried a funeral wreath with his brothers, with a wide black ribbon bearing the words, in gold letters, From Your Grandchildren. Topping the hill of the calvary — a few days before, the pastor, Balthasar Kranabeter, had stood on a stool with a paintbrush & paint bucket, retouching the flames of Hell — the sacristan, Gottfried Steinhart, carrying a cross, brought the procession to a stop. Behind the crooked purple lupins, more than a meter high, that stood in a glass vase below the floor of Hell, there was a swastika painted in pig's blood on the wall of the calvary. *Take this corpse from the trunk, and pull him to thy breast. Say these are the wounds I caused to him whom man has blessed. Wail in sorrow for thy sins, & penitence profess. Say that thou hast crucified him, and beg now to confess.*

In the clay vessel where the putrid-smelling bone stock was rendered from the bones of slaughtered animals, to be painted on the cart horses around the eyes and nostrils and on the belly, to ward off the mosquitoes and horseflies, the bone collector leaves, before it rots to nothing in the cemetery soil, the skeleton of a child killed in a tractor accident over the skeleton of Hildegard Zitterer, who died in the hospital in Villach. Did they — as is customary in the hospital — lay a stillborn infant in the coffin of Hildegard, who remained childless throughout her life, did they bury it with her, and were there two corpses in the coffin that was already sealed shut at the hospital, two in the room where her husband Willibald had previously lain exposed, an old woman and a dead infant? Not far from the overturned tractor that had crushed the child, driven by his ten-year-old brother, a horse, its iron bit covered in green saliva, shook its head, its nostrils twitching, to fend off the horseflies and mosquitoes that sucked at its oozing eyelids & damp nostrils. For a moment, the insects fled, but soon they returned to its eye sockets and nestled in its ears. Foamy green saliva dripped from the iron bit and from the horse's chin onto the grass below. The boy's corpse was carried up the steep hill to his father's farmhouse by his mother, a walking pietà, weeping and shouting her plaints into the cloudless sky. Maximilian's maternal grandfather, Matthias Felsberger, whose wife Leopoldine had already died some years before of a broken heart, because her children, aged 18, 20, and 22, fell in the war, walked back and forth for more than an hour down the village street with his bamboo cane when he heard of the news of the child killed by the tractor, trailed by the two peacocks, unapproachably lost in thought, not even once glancing over at the freshly picked snowdrops left in a mason jar at the entranceway to Hell. Maximilian walked a while at his side, tried to ask him a question — Grandpa! Grandpa! — but his grandfather would look neither left nor right and gave no answer, he just kept walking back and forth down the village street, passing by the devil with his glowing horns who bent over the sinner, relishing in his suffering, amid the crackling flames of Hell. Maximilian stayed standing beneath the red flames that shot up from Hell, smelling the freshly picked snowdrops with their scent of swamp water and molten snow. Matthias Felsberger, the agronomist, had received the two peacocks, as well as a television, in recognition of his years of service in the directorship of the Upper Carinthian dairy — it was the second television in the village, & his relatives would crowd around it once a week. This was around the time when Cassius Clay knocked out Sonny Liston. The Americans shot their rocket into space. In Dallas, John F. Kennedy's torso fell back then slumped forward in a convertible. Before the National Socialists took over, Matthias Felsberger had been mayor of the municipality of Kindelbrücken. He had already handed in his notice when the men in brown shirts stood at the door to inform him of his dismissal. I beat you to it, I've already resigned, he said to the Nazis.

The first television in the village was bought by the poorest family with the most children. Even the estate owners used to knock at their door at night, after working in the stables, to ask the fat Anita Felfernig, who would show up at the threshold, if they could watch *Löwinger-Bühne* or *Aktenzeichen XY*. Anita Felfernig was the sister-in-law of the suicide Ludmilla, who smeared her menstrual blood on the painting of Hell before hurling herself into the rapids of the Drava. In the tiny kitchen, which reeked of polenta and burnt potatoes, the television was overlaid with a brown cloth. Surrounded by six or seven pale children with deep circles under the eyes, who rarely left their house and were not allowed off the property without their parents — when they came home from working in the fields, they all sat one beside the other, as if sewn together, on the rickety hay cart — Maximilian first saw the puppet plays from Vienna's Urania theater, the stories of Kaspar and the Crocodile. Children! Caspar called, Are you there? But the children of the fat Anita, who later would die from breast cancer, said not a word throughout the night, they sat at the table gawking at the visitors and staring at the flickering blue-and-white box. When the two eldest, a boy and a girl, started primary school, and their mother took them to the schoolhouse across from the calvary with its painting of Hell, they screamed in the hallway, stomped their feet on the black wood floor, redolent of oil, tried to run out the back door, and cried so loud they could be heard from afar. Their mother and the teacher had to drag them into the classroom by force. The sons of Anita and her husband, a factory hand — he had met his wife through a classified ad in the *Carinthian Farm Journal* — turned out, with the exception of the oldest, to be smokers and drunks, & their daughters married smokers and drunks. Their eldest son, who shunned alcohol and nicotine, built a machine that would project a stamp-sized image onto the wall as big as a door. From time to time, he would bring his magic box to Maximilian's parents' and project pictures from Karl May stories onto the wall next to the pendulum clock, in the empty Biedermeyer bedroom where Maximilian's grandparents had died — the children took the pictures, along with a piece of colored chewing gum, from a little bag they had bought at the bakery in Großbotenfeld. In the darkness of the grandparents' room, they stared at Winnetou with his silver rifle, Old Shatterhand with the bear-hunter, N-tscho-tschi, Intschu-tschuna, Kleki-Petra and the rest of the Indians, at Sander & Rollins, the good guys and the bad.

The dead child's brothers carried heavy funeral wreaths on their shoulders with white paper ribbons bearing the gold inscription: A Last Goodbye! Your Brothers and Sisters. *Thou cryest, O Jesus! Be greeted, noble tears! O drops from the sea, with kisses I revere! For mine and for my neighbors' sins, they flood, my savior's tears and sacred blood. It warms the Christian's heart to see his redeemer feels no pain.* The grandmother of the unfortunate, who lived to nearly a hundred, gathered together the scattered flowers in the mortuary chapel at the foot of the sealed wooden coffin, small & white, its four corners decorated with lacquered gold angels' wings, and used them as bookmarks in her prayer book, which was held together by a thick red rubber ring like the gaskets in the lids of canning jars, so the forget-me-nots and snapdragons and prayer cards and penitence cards collected over the course of a century wouldn't slip out from the grimy, musty devotional. This devotional was placed, along with decades' worth of four-leaf clovers, pressed flat, desiccated, & browned from time, and yellowed prayer cards and penitence cards, in the hundred-year-old woman's coffin, and buried a few meters from her grandchild, who was killed in an accident, in the Catholic cemetery in Traigal, with the better part of the population in attendance.

IN THE CLAY VESSEL where the putrid-smelling bone stock was rendered from the skeletons of slaughtered animals, to be brushed on the horses with a crow's feather, around the eyes and nostrils and on the belly, to protect them from the flies and horseflies that pestered them and sucked their blood, lies the skeleton of the pastor Balthasar Kranabeter — the painter of prayer cards and images of Hell — who lay exposed for days in the church in Pulsnitz, over the skeleton of the five-year-old child, dead from a tractor accident. His head was said to be so dreadfully disfigured that his mother, who identified him, had it covered with flowers when they laid him in the coffin. They took down the papier-mâché wings that had been painted with gold lacquer and threw them over the white coffin, with wreaths and bouquets of flowers. One of the angels' wings stayed hanging from the right side, and the other from the left of the white coffin. The attendants threw clods of earth over the papier-mâché wings and the white coffin with a small pointed shovel & splashed holy water in the grave with a bristly twig. The angels carried the dead child to heaven and left him in the Mother of God's lap, as the pastor said in his sermon before the open grave, in the Catholic cemetery of Tragail, long before his own death.

The light brown wood coffin in which the Most Reverend Father Balthasar Kranabeter reposed, unadorned on a catafalque in the middle of the church, had a peephole at which the acolytes and children from the village stood on tiptoe, to once again observe his yellowed face, angular in death. Maximilian still remembers the dead man's sunken cheeks and his remarkably crooked nose. Between the lid of the coffin and its underside, a white death shroud poked out. There was a bouquet of white carnations atop it, tied with white nylon ribbons. In front of the coffin, surrounded by four lit candles, were two wreaths. The ribbon of one of them, which read A Last Goodbye, The Mayor of Kindelbrücken, bore the colors of the Carinthian flag, and the other, stating A Last Goodbye, From Your Parishioners, employing the formal mode of address with the cadaver, was purple. Candles burned on the altar as well. The tabernacle was closed. On the lace-trimmed altar cloth on which a gilded chalice stood covered by a purple cloth, Man! Here is your savior! was embroidered in gothic letters with red thread. Balthasar Kranabeter, as his obituary stated, served more than twenty-nine years as a zealous shepherd of souls in the parish of Pulsnitz. His mortal remains were taken to Upper Austria & buried in the cemetery of his birthplace, alongside his parents & brother. Maximilian's father and others among the townspeople took the train from Carinthia to Upper Austria and carried the deceased on their shoulders to his final resting place. *The savior has baptized us, we share his grave. Strange to us now are the world and its ways. Let us reject the bequest our father Adam left us through his sin, that we may find ourselves blessed in welcoming our Lord Christ in.*

The pastor had his paintings of the saints printed as prayer cards, and he would place them in the stiff, yellow hands, blue-fingertipped & cold, of the dead children and dead adults, between the rosary and the crucifix, when he gave them their final blessings with holy water and frankincense. Sometimes the prayer cards, which mostly showed the Mother of God with the child Jesus or the child Jesus by himself, bearing resemblance to some boy from the village, were left, after confession, on the grave mound of someone who had died a few weeks before, among the freshly picked carnations, until the moist, oily cemetery dirt had eaten the image away and only the eyes & forehead of Christ remained, then just the starred blue sky in the background, and finally nothing more than a few scraps of damp paper, stained with cemetery dirt. The prayer cards depicting Hell, as on the calvary in the center of the village, were given out at Easter, after confession, to those who had sinned gravely, and only to adults, never children; and the former, after repenting of their sins, handed back the little creased and frayed picture in the sacristy and received another one to keep in return, with the image of the Christ child and the mother of God. *Toi qui fais au proscrit ce regard calme et haut, Qui damne tout un peuple autour d'un échafaud. Ô Satan, prends pitié de ma longue misère!* This picture of Hell, shouted Balthasar Kranabeter from the pulpit during a sermon, has passed through practically every hand in this godless village! Woe unto you all! No more masks in God's house, no more makeup on the faces of god-fearing women, join not hands with painted nails in prayer, no more blond hair styled and rolled up in magazines, not in God's house, no! Pretty on the outside, rotten within! Woe unto you! The tainted soul would be cleansed of sin if the believer, kneeling before the altar with the prayer card in his hands, prayed ten Our Fathers and three Hail Marys, gazing penitently at the high flames among which, a fat green serpent wrapped around his naked torso, the profaner of Christ lay in torment, praying to

Father Abraham, while the crab-red devil, his wings unfurled, thick horns sprouting from his head, spilled gall into his mouth. Abraham can be seen standing at the door of Heaven with his long beard, the similarly long-bearded Lazarus kneels before him and raises his pleading hands to Abraham's breast. Father Abraham! The sinner cried, laid out on the floor of Hell, Father Abraham, take pity on me, send me to Lazarus! Let him dip his fingertips in water & freshen my tongue, for I am in great torment among these flames. Abraham answered him: Yours was a happy life and Lazarus' a hard one; now Lazarus is solaced and you are in anguish, because you broke the Son of Man to pieces. A deep chasm divides us. None of us can go to you and none of you can come to us. This was written in Gothic script in the calvary and in Roman letters under the towering flames on the prayer card. Not one of his sacred paintings, portraying Saint Christopher or the angel with the sword, did the pastor hang in the church, nor in the sacristy nor in the church vestibule. A few he gave to his friends or to his family doctor or to a young baker. Maximilian's grandfather, Matthias Felsberger, also received a framed picture, of a child's head with blond locks, two golden wings painted just below his neck. The rest of them could be found in the various rooms of the parish house, in the kitchen, the living room, and the workroom, in the cook's bedroom and in the entranceway, beside the whitish-gray, armless Jesus on the wall, his arms broken off from when he tumbled over a waterfall. The blasphemer who cast down the Son of Man will never leave Hell, according to the priest, he is damned and lost forever! God be with him. And with his soul. Amen.

Once the pastor, during a Saturday religion lesson in the schoolhouse, slowly dictated a passage of the Gospel to Maximilian & had him write it out in chalk on the blackboard. Maximilian's classmates were supposed to copy the phrase on the chalkboard in their religion notebooks, which were adorned with eyes of God, flames of purgatory, shining advent wreaths and colored crucifixes. After Maximilian had written a number of sentences on the blackboard, the priest interrupted his dictation, scrutinized the hieroglyph, and said: You can read a person's character in his script! With a raised index finger, brown from cigarette smoke, he stressed the word character several times. — Draw a cross after the last line! — Maximilian pressed the long white chalk into the black surface of the board and traced the vertical of the cross. When he began to draw the horizontal, starting from the left, the chalk broke where the two beams should have met. A chunk of chalk dropped to the freshly mopped wood floor, dark and redolent of turpentine; little bits crumbled and fell over his black shoes. The reverend looked over the heads of the children, buried in their religion notebooks, through the classroom window, to the calvary outside, in front of which stood a mason jar with plastic pink and yellow roses that the children had pulled from the rotting wreaths in the cemetery's trash heap and left below the head of the afflicted lying among the flames of Hell, who cried out and raised his hands to heaven. When Maximilian tried to erase the cross with a damp sponge, Balthasar Kranabeter snatched it from his hand & said: Lick your pathetic cross off the chalkboard! Legs spread and knees quivering, Maximilian leaned slightly forward, stuck out his tongue, and licked the white chalk cross from the board. Blushing, his teeth chattering softly, with the taste of chalk on his tongue and palate, he walked weak-kneed back to his bench, following the pastor's orders, and gripped the worn-down green seat in his damp hands. Balthasar Kranabeter raised his right hand silently and, with his finger stained brown from cigarette smoke, its nail bent, pointed out the window. The children turned their close-cropped heads. His eyes foggy, heart pounding and his head on fire — at that moment he was running a fever of thirty-nine or forty degrees — Maximilian stared a long time at the blurred flames of Hell & the green snake that wound around the naked torso and choked its victim. *Thy word shines through the dark, to Heaven lights the way. Lord, sear thy words in my heart, that I may come to thee, I pray.*

With a piece of pork still warm from the recent slaughter — the bone burner had gathered up the loose bones for the bone stock — Maximilian went out in the middle of a blizzard, after dark had already fallen, up the sawdust-covered path to the parish house and the frozen steps that led to the entrance, and pressed the glowing red doorbell. The parish cook walked past Christ's wooden torso, cracked and armless, on the corridor wall, and opened the door. Mom sent this! Maximilian said, passing the cook the fresh pork. Wait here a minute! the parish cook said. Maximilian stayed at the threshold until the cook returned from the kitchen, passed by armless Jesus — catkins hung on the wall behind Jesus' bowed head — and gave him a bag of homemade cookies. Sometimes, when they had slaughtered chickens or a cow, and Maximilian's father was feuding with the pastor and refused to send him a pair of chicken legs or a cut of beef, Maximilian, as head acolyte, fearing for his special position in the church, would beg his mother when his father was away, until she wrapped a piece of meat in wax paper and sent him off with it. A little meat for the pastor and his maid, Mama, it doesn't have to be a big piece! At times, in winter, when the hill of the parish house was especially icy, Maximilian would get a basket of sawdust from his parents' hayloft and scatter it over the path, because the priest always complained in the religion class of his fear that, going down the icy hill of the parish house to conduct the six AM mass, when it was still pitch-black in the village, he might one day fall down and break his leg.

One Sunday morning, when Balthasar Kranabeter was walking down the hill of the parish house to mass — purple and lilac-colored crocuses and white carnations bloomed on the mossy slope — he ran into Maximilian's father, holding a whip and waiting on the bridge for the thirsty cows, their noses sunk in the trough, before driving them out to pasture. So you mind your cows instead of going to church! Balthasar Kranabeter reproached him. You take the whip, Father, and I'll go to church and you can drive the cows out to pasture! Maximilian's father said, and took his cows down the village street, passing alongside the calvary — to the left and right of the image of Hell blossomed meter-high yellow laburnum, surrounded by buzzing bees — over the slope of the pond, to the fertile green. A child with peacock feathers in his headband angled his bicycle around the hot and smoking mounds of fallen dung.

One time, at eight in the morning, when Maximilian's mother went to mass, entering the church through the broad black back door, over the threshold of which they carried out the coffins and the married couples stepped and the little brides of Christ, in their white dresses, walked into the house of God to take their first communion, the paſtor, seated on the acolytes' narrow black bench at the entrance of the sacriſty, turned his head toward the woman. He interrupted his silent prayer, ſtood up, went into the sacriſty, & had the bald, toothless sacriſtan, who had already lit the candles on the alter, dress him for mass. He thundered from the pulpit during the sermon: You need not give the prieſt an extra drop of milk! When she heard these words, Maximilian's mother said, she wanted to ſtand up in the middle of mass & walk out. Every day she had poured milk into the milk jug for the parish cook well over the liter line & she had only charged them for a liter a day.

In the woodshed of the affiliate church in Paulinenhorſt, where he miniſtered once a month, Balthasar Kranabeter singlehandedly hacked to pieces an altar that had been changed out for another one, valuable both as a work of art and as an antique — This is kitsch! — and left it as firewood. How could he juſt hack up an altar! At that point I took fright of the prieſt and I've kept away from him since! the sacriſtan's wife lamented, when Maximilian knocked recently at the door of her house to ask her to lend him the church keys. After decades, he wanted again to see the altar and the sacriſty where he had put on his acolyte's dress, several times a year, when he used to ride with the prieſt and his cook in a white Volkswagen.

When the reverend saw the tomb of Maximilian's grandfather, Florian Kirchheimer, which they had just finished constructing, he stood shaking his head behind the creaking gate, and yelled Kitsch! Kitsch! Kitsch! Shaking his head and muttering to himself, he walked along the paved path between the graves toward the sacristy and had himself dressed for mass by his toothless, wheezing, bandy-legged servant Oswin, who had already pulled the bell rope to call the town to mass. When the sacristan Gottfried Steinhart was ill, Oswin not only pulled the rope, but also lit the candles on the altar and helped the priest put on & take off his vestments.

After saying mass, Balthasar Kranabeter walked back over the paved path between the graves with the church key, from which a wooden cross dangled, through the creaking gate of the cemetery and slowly down the village street in the direction of the parish house. He paused a moment at the calvary, before the reflections in the schoolhouse windows. In a vase were six or seven peacock feathers, some short, others long. The blue eyes of three feathers grazed the red flames and hid the head of the afflicted, who twisted amid the fires of Hell, wrestling with the devil and with the green serpent that was as thick as a man's arm. *Toi qui sais en quels coins des terres envieuses, Le Dieu jaloux cacha les pierres précieuses, Ô Satan, prends pitié de ma longue misère!*

The wooden cross on the church keys rubbed against the right seam of the servant of God's pants leg as he passed by a humming beehive redolent of honeycomb. The peacocks' cries, strident and metallic, broke the town's silence, reverberating down into the marrow. Scarcely ten minutes later, the parish cook, with the dusty purple curtain of the confessional draped over her naked right forearm, walked down the village street, crossing herself as she passed the calvary on her way to the parish house.

In late summer, Maximilian often went with the parish cook into the forest, where he would learn to distinguish among the edible, the savory, the unpalatable, and the poisonous mushrooms, because in his parents' farmhouse they were so afraid of being poisoned that they hadn't eaten any mushrooms for decades. That's a devil's mushroom, she said, pay attention, it looks like an angel's mushroom. The devil's mushroom is deadly! If you squeeze a devil's mushroom, it turns blue. If you squeeze an angel's mushroom, it won't change color. That's how you tell a devil's mushroom from an angel's. Angel's mushrooms are the ones the priest likes the most, she said. In late afternoon they arrived with a basket of chanterelles, porcini and parasols, a bundle of herbs, raspberries, blueberries and even lingonberries at the cool parish house. Balthasar Kranabeter was seated with a paintbrush in his hand at an easel in the shadows of the backyard, painting a new religious piece. The cook left the basket, with the angel's mushrooms' brown spongy caps and the delicious-smelling parasols poking out over its braided edge, under the already crumbling fresco the priest had painted on the parish house wall. Jesus be praised! said the pastor, dipping his paintbrush in the red-stained water. For ever & ever, amen! his acolyte responded.

Klaus Hafner, of the Catholic faith, was married in the Protestant church. When his Catholic father died, he wished to have him buried in the Catholic cemetery in Pulsnitz, but as the son of the deceased had married in the Protestant church, the religious painter and pastor refused to give the final blessings to his Catholic parents in the Catholic cemetery in Pulsnitz. A Protestant minister accompanied them to their final resting place. Later, Klaus Hafner, who poisoned himself on the banks of the Drava in Pulsnitz with the gas from the exhaust pipe of his car, would be buried alongside his parents in the Protestant cemetery, in the tomb of his sixteen-year-old son Roman. His son preceded him, hanging himself some years before in Pulsnitz, in the hayloft of his rachitic uncle, Otmar Hafner, with a calf-halter, it is thought.

WHEN MS. LAKONIG went on her bicycle through the outstretched right arm of the village built in the form of a cross, to the Steinharts' — Jonathan, that family's seventeen-year-old son, had hanged himself with his friend Leopold, of the same age, a few years before — to pick up fresh milk, still warm from the cow, for the evening meal, she was struck by a truck that swerved onto the shoulder of the road. She flew with her bicycle past an elderberry, its black umbels hanging low, down the hill into a poppy-covered wheat field. When a retired bricklayer told her husband, Wilfried Lakonig, that his wife lay dead in a furrow in a wheat field, the man screamed into the handpiece: Fuck off! Pack her up and get her to the morgue! The retiree who shared the bad news had lost a son himself a few years before, in Egypt, also in a traffic accident. Two jeeps had collided on a desert road...

The black hearse with the silver cross in the milk glass of the windows, belonging to Sonnberger from Großbotenfeld, was called to the scene of the accident by the police, and arrived at the same time as the coroner. Two men in gray coats, one young and one old, stepped out from a Mercedes and heaved the woman's bloody and disfigured corpse into a gray metal coffin at the edge of the wheat field. When the funeral procession, led by the sacristan with a crucifix, neared the center of the village and the schoolhouse, the peacock, standing at the calvary, the fan of its outstretched tail feathers covering the flames and the naked torso of the screaming blasphemer who lay on the floor of Hell, took flight, whipping its tail feathers a few centimeters above the asphalted street. Only Lucifer's horned scalp had been visible over the eyes of its feathers, with his unfurled red wings and his claws spilling gall into the sinner's mouth. The dusty undersides of a few haggard eyeless feathers brushed the ground when the peacock, startled by the black coil of the procession, took off over the village street, hiding under the gangway of the Felsbergers' barn and settling into the hot, dusty earth. There was no bouquet of delicate posies, quickly expiring under the violently flickering flames, only the shards of a shattered vase lay there. No red bouquets of poppies were tied to the coffin, not even a bundle of green poppy seed pods when they lowered the casket with a creaking rope into the deep earth. A large bouquet of red carnations hid the small wooden cross, light brown, with its plastic Jesus nailed into the coffin lid. Instead of taking the aspergil from the copper dish of holy water, Katharina, the mother of the young suicide Jonathan — she was a friend, the deceased had perished on the way to her house to pick up milk — splashed the coffin, already in the grave, with milk from a medicine bottle, and was led to her farmhouse just after the burial by two men, one young & one old, a father and a son, who walked at her right and left, holding her up by her arms.

In the clay vessel where the putrid-smelling bone stock was rendered from the bones of slaughtered animals, to be brushed on the horses with a crow's feather, around the eyes and nostrils and on the belly, to protect them from the mosquitoes and horseflies, the skeleton of the deceased lies over the skeleton of the pastor & religious painter who, as he had preceded her in death, was unable to give her his final blessing; the mortal remains of the shepherd of souls were driven in a black Mercedes from Carinthia to Upper Austria, by the same people who took the woman's corpse, found in a wheat field with countless broken bones, from Pulsnitz to the morgue in Großbotenfeld. A few weeks later, the combine, painted green like an iron insect, was in the valley shoving ears of grain into its maws and leaving one tract of stubble after another in its wake. Not far away, a few meters from where the cadaver had lain with the bicycle and the empty milk can, the half-naked farm children wearing ski goggles, a film of gray dust over their tan bodies, were tying up the full grain bags in the hot, dry afternoon, and throwing them from the combine onto the stubble field. *Hail, O Queen of Heaven enthroned. Hail, by angels mistress owned. Root of Jesse, gate of morn, whence the world's true light was born: glorious Virgin, joy to thee, loveliest whom in heaven they see; fairest thou, where all are fair, plead with Christ our souls to spare.*

AFTER VISITING THE DEATHBED, the man with the gray-flecked moustache & trimmed brows, seventy years old at the time, entered the kitchen with reddened eyes, hung his hat on the red porcelain knob of the coat tree, where a switch of a hazel also rested, and told his family, in a plaintive tone, that his best friend in the village, the diminutive, rachitic farmer Hafner, had died at seventy in the hospital in Villach. A few years before his death, the sacristan had left a pile of dung on his doorstep over a page from the weekly *Carinthian Farm Journal*. That night Otmar Hafner, suspecting none other than the sacristan Gottfried Steinhart, with whom he had an ongoing feud, picked up the copy of the *Carinthian Farm Journal* with its load of human feces, crossed the street of the village, walked through the neighbor's yard and left it at the door of the presumed offender. Since then, the dwarfish, rachitic farmer said, he runs away from me, he hides in his house or in the stable whenever we cross paths. Maybe the next morning, when he got up to go to the church and ring the bell, he stepped in his own shit, he mused with a toothless grin. It wasn't until his sixth year, Maximilian's father said, that the rachitic Otmar began to walk, before that he used to drag himself along the floor of his parents' house. All the sudden one day, said the ninety-year-old man with the gray-flecked moustache and the trimmed brows, the boy got up and walked.

Hafner's nephew, the sixteen-year-old Roman, whose bones lie below the skeleton of his rachitic uncle in the clay vessel where the pandapigl was rendered from the bones of slaughtered animals, to be brushed on the horses around the eyes and nostrils and on the belly, to protect them from mosquitoes & horseflies, began the cycle of suicides in the village of Maximilian's birth. In front of the barn, standing near the head of the horse harnessed to the hay cart, Roman would grab hold of the reins. Foamy green spit mixed with fresh-chewed grass dripped from the grooved iron bit and onto the back of the boy's hand. With a hazel switch in his other hand, he would flog the horse's shimmering black legs, where horseflies had landed and were feeding. The horse would draw back its bulging, blue-black upper lip, showing its long yellow teeth, and, with its eyes bulging out, ringed with the black bone stock, its ears stiff and pointed, the veins in its legs swelling with the effort, it would pull the hay cart up the creaking gangway and into the dark barn smelling of freshly reaped hay, while the young man ran at its side gripping the reins. The sixteen-year-old Roman, who would one day have taken charge of his uncle's small holdings, used to go down the village street to his uncle's farm after work; he'd get out of his boss's company car where the two beams of the cross-shaped town met. He never said a timid prayer in front of the Calvary, nor would he leave forget-me-nots or catkins before the sea of flames, nor did he go to the pastor's religion classes, he was a Protestant, a Lutheran, according to the townspeople. They ought to turn Hell upside down, he used to say, particularly when people would ask him why they never saw him there among the images of saints who warmed men's souls in the Catholic church. He didn't go to the Catholic festivals either; he met other children & teenagers only when they kicked a soccer ball around among the cows that grazed on his uncle's land. At fourteen, he could already be found out at the bars, sitting with a Villach beer and smoking a cigarette. His father and his older brother also drank & smoked. After clearing the manure from the stables, watering the cows and calves, and giving the cat a little milk — scraps of straw bobbed in the cat's dung-splattered bowl — he used to go, when he wasn't sleeping at his uncle's, to his parents' house on the edge of the village, a good kilometer away, carrying in his leather satchel the balled-up paper full of bread crumbs that had held his lunch as well as a jug of fresh milk, still warm from the cow. Roman's nephew said that once, after he was done with work and had dropped off the fresh milk, he asked his sister-in-law, who also lived at his parents', to make him a ham and cheese sandwich; but there was no bread left in the house, & she couldn't make him anything. That night, Roman left his parents' house forever. When he'd been gone for two days, and his brothers and parents had sought him out in vain, his dwarfish and rachitic uncle Otmar opened the barn door, saw the boy dangling from a rope tied to a beam, and cried: There he hangs!

Over the skeleton of the rachitic farmer Hafner and the skeleton of his nephew Roman lie the bones of Roman's father, Klaus Hafner, in the clay vessel where the pandapigl was rendered from the bones of slaughtered animals, to be brushed on the horses around the eyes and nostrils and on the belly, to protect them from the mosquitoes and horseflies. A few years after the young man's suicide, his father also took his own life. In the weeks before his corpse was discovered in the backseat of a Volkswagen parked along the banks of the Drava, full of exhaust fumes that had been piped into the car with a garden hose, a passerby, thinking it strange that a parked car was running, had saved his life. The car was locked and fogged over inside. The passerby broke out the window and the acrid exhaust fumes streamed out. He opened the door, grabbed the arm of the man, who was strapped in unconscious behind the steering wheel, and tried to pull him out. Then he ran around the car, flung open the other door, and unfastened the seatbelt.

The second suicide attempt succeeded along the desolate shores of the Drava. For years afterward, the interior of the Volkswagen smelled of the deadly exhaust fumes. It was always a torment for me, having to get into that car as a child, Roman's nephew said, I would think over and over of my grandfather's killing himself on the shores of the Drava and of my uncle, hanging dead from a rafter. My grandmother and my parents almost never talked about it. Anyone who brought it up they called a downer. Though the father and son were both buried in the mountains, in the Protestant cemetery rather than in the Catholic one in Pulsnitz, the black Mercedes still drove by the calvary with the corpses, up the village street to the morgue in Großbotenfeld. On the left and right of the hood of the black Mercedes were two flags bearing images of Hell. The red flames fluttered in the draft. The accursed devil dumped out his gall, but as the car drove by, the contents of the cup could not reach the mouth of the afflicted, who lay on the floor of Hell, calling out to Father Abraham. The serpent's tongue, hissing and sputtering, was coated with soot from the restless flames fed by the draft. *Toi dont la large main cache les précipices, Au somnambule errant au bord des édifices, Ô Satan, prends pitié de ma longue misère!* The mother of the one suicide and wife of the other, a prematurely old and wrinkled woman, had — like Maximilian's mother — lost three of her brothers, in the full flower of youth, on the battlefields of the Second World War.

It was in the Hafners' shack that Maximilian, then five or six, first saw a mourning chamber, with black cloths and electric candles, after the death of the rachitic farmer's grandmother, who was also buried in the Protestant cemetery in the mountains in Blitzbergen.

Maximilian, in worn-out leather short pants, his knees crusted in blood, sat on a fence under the branches of the plum tree and bit into the pulp of a blue plum while the casket and the wreaths were packed into a cattle trailer. The mourners and family members crouched around the casket among the wreaths. With a rumble, the cattle trailer set to motion, the coffin slid a half-meter and the people seated around it grabbed onto each other's shirtsleeves.

RECENTLY THE MOTHER of Roman, the boy who brought his life to an end in the barn of his rachitic uncle with a harness of the kind used to drag calves into the world, sat on the bus beside a neighbor who used to go daily to the graveside of her grandson, killed in an accident at five years of age. The two women leaned their heads together, their faces deeply furrowed, when they saw Maximilian take his seat behind them. Maximilian was not even ten when he had run into a schoolmate in a shop who told him, unsettled, that a boy had been *squashed* in the neighboring village of Römerhof. Maximilian ran through the street, passing by the power station, descended the hill, and saw from the distance a group of people gathered in a roadside field. On the shoulder of the road, the five-year-old child had slipped from the grasp of his grandmother — the same one who would sit in front of Maximilian on the bus decades later

— & been struck by an oncoming car and was thrown through the air in a high arc, over the frightened, screaming woman's head, into the clover field where he lay with a broken neck. Helpless and heaving, the doctor knelt before the body, took the boy's pulse and confirmed he was no longer breathing, closed his brown doctor's bag, and laid packing paper over the boy's blood-smeared head. Over and over he took the boy's pulse and dropped his hand despondently in the grass. The horrified grandmother, in a severe state of shock, stared at the little bare feet that poked out from the packing paper and pressed a wrinkled kerchief with shivering hands against her trembling lower jaw. A helper, surrounded by onlookers, wrapped the boy's lifeless body in the brown paper and took the corpse to his parents' house, fewer than a hundred steps from the scene of the accident. The torn nylon suspenders of the dead child danced in rhythm to the footsteps, grazing the grass & gravel along the way. His shoes lay somewhere out in the field.

For three days the child lay in his parents' house, surrounded by spring flowers, narcissus, tulips, and Christmas roses, in a sealed coffin, small & white. Maximilian's mother had packed a wicker basket with Linde coffee, Melanda coffee, and a kilogram of sugar cubes and had gone to the viewing the following night, after working in the stable and feeding the pigs. Pale, with blue lips and her eyes glazed over, her eyelids swollen and red, she came back two hours later and tapped on the kitchen window. Maximilian closed his Karl May book and opened the front door. She didn't speak a word, she made dinner for her children, milk-coffee and polenta, washed the dishes and went to her room, where a newborn was breathing in an oval-shaped wicker basket in front of a ceramic stove beside her bed.

The burial took place three days after the accident. The white coffin with its four white angel wings of braided wire, moving in rhythm with the footsteps, was carried by four teenagers, white-clothed and freshly shaven, through the village street, passing by the schoolhouse and the calvary in the direction of the church. Under the vibrant red flames leaping up from Hell, a yellow beeswax candle burned, giving off a great quantity of soot. Beside it lay the wrapper from a book of matches from the Sirius match factory in Klagenfurt & a prayer card with red and yellow flames. A white flag, fluttering fretfully, was tied to the right biceps of the Crucified, whom the sacristan Steinhart carried on a long staff at the head of the procession. A group of children with lit candles whispering continuously to one another picked the hot candlewax off their fingers and followed the pastor Balthasar Kranabeter, dressed in black & praying aloud, flanked by two acolytes in black and white who carried the censer and the hammered copper aspersorium. The wind pressed the black mourning veil against the face of the child's grandmother. Many of the candles were blown out, and the parish cook relit them with Sirius matches. The peacocks were not to be seen. Partridges and pheasants ran through the fields behind the orchards, took flight, and alighted elsewhere. The hunchback servant Oswin, toothless & gasping, pulled the bell rope in the sacristy when the funeral procession neared the open cemetery gate. The next day, after the matins, Balthasar Kranabeter sat on a stool, meticulously wiping the soot from the beeswax candle off of the red flames leaping up from the floor of Hell, with a cloth that he dipped in a chemical solution. *Not Isaac, but the son of God, perished for our good! Mercifully he looked on as they nailed him to the wood. And we sinners complain when our way comes a mote of earthly strife? The crosses we bear lead us to despair, we know not that they promise eternal life.*

By the cross she stands, tears on her cheeks, desperate and alone, her heart pierced through by the dying cries of her only begotten son. After Jonathan, wearing only his pajamas, jumped out of his bedroom window in the middle of the night & met with Leopold, who awaited him in the garden, the two went to the stable and put a three-meter-long hemp rope in a bricklayer's bag splattered with quicklime. On a September night, under the light of the moon, they walked with the rope up the village street, passing the calvary, not noticing the devil's red wings, which were stretched to the point of tearing — Lucifer was sweating blood — and then up the hill of the parish house into the barn. In the empty barn full of dusty cobwebs — the parish house was unoccupied at the time — they climbed a wooden ladder to the crossbeam. The two boys tied the two ends of rope behind their ears and jumped into the emptiness, weeping and embracing, a few meters from the armless Christ who had once been rescued from a stream bed by the priest and painter of prayer cards and who now stood in the entranceway of the parish house, gasping and smelling the blood sweated out by the devil in the calvary. With their tongues out, their sexes stiff, their semen-flecked pants dripping urine, Jonathan in pajamas and Leopold in his quicklime-splattered bricklayer's clothes, they hung in the barn of the parish house until they were found by Jonathan's sixteen-year-old cousin, who shined the beam of his flashlight across their four dangling legs twenty-four hours later, and were cut down with a butcher's knife by Adam the Third.

The two boys' lifeless bodies dropped to the floor of the parish barn and slumped together. Adam the Third laid the bodies in the hay, pressed their hands together, pushed their tongues back into their mouths — Leopold's was bitten off, no one, not even the police, ever found that scrap of tongue in the barn — closed their eyelids and, his heart pounding and with trembling hands, prayed for the intercession of the saints before leaving, his butcher knife still in hand, to call the police; finally, taking the crossroads from his house to

Jonathan's parents', he knocked at the kitchen door & stood horrified at the threshold, his arms outstretched, his eyes wide open and his mouth agape. No words were necessary, the disaster was written on his face. The eyes of Jonathan's mother Katherine fogged over. She knew what to do to be close to her son, to feel his presence. She turned in a circle, elegantly, at first, with her hands extended, before taking leave of her senses and falling with a bang, like a marionette with its cords cut, to the wooden floor. The afflicted was laid on the sofa, her knees bent, by Adam the Third and her husband, who sobbed loudly. *How wretched, how sorrowful, the mother of Jesus wails, as she stands before her son and sees hands pierced through by nails.* In the clay vessel where the putrid-smelling bone stock was rendered from the bones of slaughtered animals, to be brushed on the horses around the eyes and nostrils and on the belly, to ward off the mosquitoes & blackflies, the skeletons of the two suicides lie over that of a five-year-old child who, holding a bouquet of mayflowers, pulled away from his grandmother's hand on the side of the road. Maximilian, just after learning of the double suicide — the local press dedicated countless pages to that tragedy of youth, and on the radio one often heard the creaking of hemp rope, recondite explanations of knots by experts, and every hour, the cordier from the neighboring village repeating his slogan — went from Klagenfurt to Pulsnitz to the parish barn, and found a piece of rope still there.

He keeps the instrument of suicide even today, and from time to time he picks up the hemp rope & examines the depression where it once held more than one-hundred-fifty kilograms off the floor. The two halves of the rope that were tied around the boys' necks were confiscated by the police, preserved in formalin, & sent to the Vienna Crime Museum. It was horrible! said Anita Felfernig — the village's television owner and mother of seven hungry children, who would die of breast cancer a few years after the double suicide — to Maximilian, when she saw him come over the hill to the parish house & approach the scene of the disaster. Jonathan's parents only sent the blue-trimmed death notices to their closest relatives, because the townspeople were feuding, and after the deaths of Balthasar Kranabeter, the pastor and painter of prayer cards, and of Matthias Felsberger, Maximilian's dumbstruck grandfather, who had lost three sons in the full flower of youth in the Second World War, they were engulfed for years by spite, slander, and litigation.

At a meeting of neighbors in the village inn, where the landowners gathered once or twice a year to talk about the use of the shared combine and the common floodplains, the farmer Philippitsch — Adam the Third — who had taken pity on the two boys' lifeless bodies and cut them down from the heights, sprang up from his chair — a beer bottle overturned and a coaster rolled across the floor — and defamed Maximilian's father: If I listed every one of your outrages, you'd have to hide under the table in shame. In court, Adam the Third was unable to attest to any such outrages. I'll hunt you down whichever way I can! threatened Adam, who was strong as a bear, pointing with his index finger after the trial had ended. Adam's brother-in-law, whom Maximilian's father also hauled before the court, was likewise incapable of proving that the latter had stolen sacks of grain from the Philippitsch farm. Adam the Third's brother-in-law, a locksmith and a drunk — his son is a locksmith and a drunk as well — let fly on one of his benders that he had not only caught Maximilian's father red-handed stealing grain, but that he had punished the thief for this outrage, in the dusty, cobweb-cluttered mill, laying him across his knee like a rascal. I lit him up good! he boasted to the amusement of his drinking companions at the bar of the inn, lifting up — Cheers! — one glass after another of the yellow, foamy liquid, produced in Villach-on-the-Drava. After so much slander and so many trials, the farmers avoided each other whenever possible, and years passed without their exchanging a word. But if their paths crossed by chance, unexpectedly, at a funeral or on Corpus Christi, or at some church function during Holy Week — eventually they had to get in line with the villagers on Good Friday to kiss the feet of the Crucified — they stuck their heads in the sand without a word or greeting. Maximilian and his cousin held the tall cross against the closed altar rails and watched the mouths of the believers as they bent over to plant one on the nailed-together feet of Christ. They took note of who merely mimed a kiss and who actually pressed their lips against a toenail or one of the spikes in Christ's feet, as well as of those who remained shut-eyed, their heads piously bowed, several seconds before the Crucified, before standing and filing out through the black rows of pews. Maximilian's father exchanged his final words with the drunken locksmith before the court. It was not his way to say: He is nothing to me, or he is dead to me, he hardly mentioned his accuser, or perhaps never again; for him the drunk, who is now on the mend — Cheers! — was already dead and rotting even before he had suffered his first heart attack.

The ninety-year-old man with the gray-flecked moustache and the trimmed eyebrows was in the meantime informed by Hannes Walluschnig, who has since met his end as well, from cancer, that Jonathan had been made to turn over a part of his earnings to his parents when he began his mechanic's apprenticeship. Whether his parents placed this money in a savings account or used it for their own purposes was not discussed. A vicious rumor also spread through the village that, as an acolyte, Jonathan had stolen money from the collection bag, and everyone asked himself whether the thief had stolen his or someone else's ten-schilling piece. During mass, after the transubstantiation, when the pastor Balthasar Kranabeter would convert a half-chalice of Samos wine into the highly concentrated blood of

Christ, quench his thirst therewith and ingest the Most High, before administering the host to the faithful, impressed with an image of Hell, and thereby either calming their souls or distressing them further, Jonathan would pass among the rows of benches with the collection bag, giving thanks to whatever parishioner cast his alms in the red cloth bag with the golden cord and nodding his head with the phrase: May God repay you! A long pole was used to reach those of the faithful who seated themselves in the back corners, to pass the bag under their noses, & to stroke the stubbly chin of the spendthrift farmer Philippitsch with its gold-fringed hem. As children, the three daughters of Adam the Third used to stroke his black stubble with their small, tender hands before the barber laid his razor on his temples to shave it off. You should not say Thank you, you should say May God repay you! It is God who shall repay you! the pastor Balthasar Kranabeter clarified to the acolytes in the sacristy, while Maximilian and the other underlings thanked him for the five schillings he pressed into their hands in reward for their services. The acolytes knelt before the priest, the five-schilling coins in their fists, saying Praise Jesus, and exited the sacristy, after the pastor had answered their thanks with the phrase, For ever and ever, Amen! Jonathan had also complained — Hannes Walluschnig claimed — that his landowning parents found the company of his friend Leopold unbecoming, because the latter, a bricklayer's apprentice, who had to earn his room and board in a farmhouse in the village like a peasant, was the mere son of a servant couple, a maid & a menial who raised their twelve children in the outbuilding of a farmhouse that had served as lodgings for German children on vacation before Leopold & his siblings were born. Maximilian remembers that the drunken Leopold had once hugged Jonathan at the village fair, and had cried out, loud & desperate amid the din of the dancers and the noise of the brass band, You're my boyfriend! Jealous and red-faced, Maximilian left the hot, moist church tent, which smelled of cheap aftershave, bad wine, the sweat of dancers, and lukewarm Villach beer. Parish feast! you had better say, I never want to hear the word fair again, God's servant, Balthasar Kranabeter, said to his acolytes, it is a festival in honor of the Lord and his house. The house of God shall not be turned into a fairground! Not over my dead body!

Neither did Maximilian's aunt Silvia or her husband Kajetan receive the blue-trimmed death notices — they had feuded with Jonathan's parents, and didn't say a word to them for years, after Jonathan's grandfather, the sacristan, had cursed his son-in-law Kajetan: I hope you drop off like the Kohlweiß innkeeper! — but this did not keep her from flaunting her misery, she went off unbidden to Jonathan's funeral. After all, she was the suicide's aunt, his father's sister. In front of the pit where Jonathan's blue casket lay covered over with flowers — mostly

cigarettes, now with three sons to mourn, has taken up in the interim the profession of funeral director in Spittal-on-the-Drava.

She saw Jesus tied fast & pierced with a thousand wounds for the iniquity of man. She saw the son she had once nourished disgraced and abandoned, pale and thirsting on the cross. In the clay vessel where the putrid-smelling bone stock was rendered from the bones of slaughtered animals, to be painted on the horses with a black crow's feather around the eyes & nostrils and on the belly, to protect them from the mosquitoes and horseflies, the bone collector lays the skeleton of Katharina, Jonathan's mother, over the skeletons of the four suicides, among them that of Jonathan, whom she outlived by more than fifteen years. In the coffin, her hands were folded in prayer over her scarred torso, the breasts amputated by a surgeon. Her husband interlaced her fingers with a pink rosary from her pilgrimage to Lourdes, which she took up daily from the night table for more than fifteen years, almost always in the afternoon, staring out the second-floor window of her farmhouse and praying, gazing expectantly over the nearby wall of the cemetery at her child's grave, lit up by a flickering wax candle, which seemed to float and waver with the undulating flame. At times she stayed there until the wee hours of the morning, until the candle had burnt out and a pillar of smoke, ever thinner, rose up from the grave. Then Katharina would close the window and go back to her husband, already asleep for hours. *O thou Mother! fount of love! Touch my ſpirit from above, make my heart with thine accord: Make me feel as thou haſt felt; make my soul to glow & melt with the love of Chriſt my Lord.*

The tomb rose and floated over the other graves, with earth-clotted roots of red clover, went from plot to plot, looking down on the blue, yellow, and violet eyes of the pansies, and ſtaring at the yellow and red petals of the snapdragons. She winced when her son's tomb scraped againſt the cross on a gravesite, rolled back and forth in bed, and awoke with a pounding heart as it bumped againſt the cemetery wall, ſpilling clods of earth onto the ground, and the Crucified, nailed to the lid of the blue coffin, vomited up cemetery dirt. Then Katharina threw off the cover, ſtood up, went to the window, lifted her binoculars to eye-height and looked out into the cemetery. The candle on the grave-mound had given out some time ago. The sky quiet & ſtar-dotted. The grain fields pitch-black. The cemetery breathed in silently. Even the ruſtle of the birch-leaves, threaded together with ſpider-webs, was inaudible. The river looped soundlessly by. Mangy cats curled up in the holy corners of the farmhouses and the dogs slept, paws covering their muzzles. Not even a mole's eye glimmered, nor were there fireflies to be seen. The bell rope, which hung wavering in the sacriſty, turned into a serpent, slithered up the ſteeple, and beat its head againſt the belfry until its cold snake's blood ran slowly down the bell rope and dripped on the sacristy floor. Atop the steeple, bats thrashed in silence, stretched their wings, opened their maws, and folded the thin, nearly transparent skin of their wings anew over their black bodies. The host with the image of Hell impressed on it shattered the body of Christ. A drop of blood danced in the candle in the sanctuary. The baptismal font, where the newly born were commended unto Christ, teemed with green tree frogs nailed to miniature hobbyhorses. He always liked to take them in his hand, those little grass-green beasts that hop out of your palm, sometimes he would step on them and wipe their innards off his shoes in the grass. He had also liked to feed breadcrumbs to the raven whose wings we clipped, he used to give it water, and he tore out its silver-shining eyes. How many times he had gone to the calvary to cut at the leaping flames of Hell, until the scissors, soot-blackened, were burning, and he threw them into the yellow bush of blossoming laburnum. Who has come & gone, who has gathered up the periwinkles and piled them up in secret behind the calvary? Is the bulb still burning in front of the house? Forever and ever I shall take care that a milk glass bulb, and only milk glass, is screwed into the socket, so the shadows of the insects are visible around it, wriggling and dying with their long, thin legs. Don't leave fingerprints on the iron latch of the cemetery gate because, who knows, maybe the Adversary will steal them in the night and hide them in his calvary behind the spiderwebs. Who knows whether the screaming blasphemer, laid out on the floor of Hell, who once threw a statue of Christ over a cliff into a stream bed, holds the sooty periwinkles in the fists of his raised arms, and if the white cat hopping in the snow has licked up the blood drops from the torn angels' wings? The fog lifts and falls, it haunts us, it comes from the shores of the Drava, the hair of the girls is damp as they pass up the village street, carrying freshly picked lilies of the valley, and pass nervously by the calvary. If only the wind would stop rustling the pages of the prayer book night after night, closing them & rustling through them and closing them again, slamming them shut! Then I could sleep better, but I keep hearing a rustle, a rifling, a crackle, a gust, and I do not know, is it the stream, is it paper burning into ash, is it the East Wind bearing a storm, or the flames of Hell drawn on a sheet of blotting paper. At least the boys splashed each other with holy water in the sacristy and took a host from the tabernacle, even if it wasn't yet blessed, with the image of the calvary and its depiction of Hell pressed into it, and assimilated Christ's body, splitting it in half, the one carrying the profaner of Christ in his stomach, the other the devil, before they walked past their parents' house, past the calvary, past everywhere, past, past, going nimbly up to the place of their death. Katharina closed her eyes, set the binoculars soundlessly on the windowsill, breathed in the scent of the grain fields, and opened up her eyes. She shut the window, stared wide-eyed at the contours of her pitch-black shadow in the window-pane, turned, walking over the softly creaking wooden floor, and lay in bed beside her sleeping husband. *Holy Mother! pierce me through, in my heart each wound renew of my Savior crucified: Let me share with thee His pain, who for all my sins was slain, who for me in torments died.*

For more than fifteen years, his mother Katharina would go to the cemetery at the call for prayers & place a candle in a red grave lantern painted with sacred hearts pierced by arrows, striking a match against the box labeled Sirius. Every day for more than fifteen years she hoped her seventeen-year-old son would throw back the turf of the graveyard like a bedcover, stand up, wipe the clumped, sticky soil, smelling of the countless dead, from his blue suit, & pin on a slightly withered plastic carnation, before approaching through the darkness the eternally burning porch light of his parents' home, which would serve to guide him in case, confused from lying so long beneath the earth, he no longer recognized the house where he was born. She hoped he would knock one day, not on the door of the stable, but on his parents' door, asking permission to enter, & would wet his finger in the bowl of holy water held at eye-level by a porcelain angel. *Humbly Father have thy children entered in thy den, to worship thee in spirit, to confess to thee their sins.*

We recognize our failings, in atonement do we bow; in thy name, we shall live again, have mercy, do not cast us out. He will return. He will kneel down, he will bow his head. He will cross himself & fold his hands in prayer, and he will recite the guardian angel prayer with me. Ever this day be at my side, to light and guard, to rule and guide.

It was all for nothing, he is not risen, although year after year, on Corpus Christi, & not only in dreams, I have tied a crawfish to a red candle. The long, thin feelers of the crawfish, its protuberant eyes and its claws, were overrun with the hot wax draining from the candle, until its frantic claws and feelers moved ever slower and the dying crustacean, embalmed in red wax, fell still inside his tomb. I caught a thousand crawfish in a fishing net and put them alive into a rock pool. I wanted to take a live one every day to Jonathan's grave and tie it to a lit candle, but my dead son, in God's name, emptied out the rock pool and pulled the nails from my fingers while I was sleeping, while my hands lay over the bedcover tangled up in my rosary. With my fingers still bloody and oozing, I undid the knots in the fishing net and set all the crawfish free. In the morning, when I awoke, the pink Lourdes rosary lay blood-smeared on the floor beside the night table. Who knows who closed the prayer book, bound in black fabric, impressed with a golden cross, then opened it back up, then closed it again. Perhaps he came for me and stole away with the four-leaf clover bookmark. It was cold out. Fog lay over the graves. The riverside forest hid itself away. The bent black candlewick was stiff — I saw it through the binoculars — it had frozen through. Three or four times already, the peacocks had opened their beaks and noiselessly swallowed their cries. The weathervane on the church tower spun in the air, swirling up the dust of God. The poplars bowed, their leaves swishing and rustling. Smoking chimneys spewed out small, almost invisible particles of soot. It smelled of burnt beechwood. The farm people had retired to their bedrooms, beside the tiled stoves, to stare at the flickering images on the blue TV screen. Around the gray felt slippers, cats purred. Inside the felt slippers, swastikas were embroidered with black thread. A skeleton, a Thanksgiving crown on his head, marched along a rainbow and introduced the next film. The roaring lion from Metro Goldwyn Mayer burst into the village & swallowed the armless Christ in the entranceway to the parish house whole. In the black eye sockets of the dead, and over the thousands of molehills spread throughout the plains, the snow fell noiselessly. Only the bandy-legged wolf, wandering over my footprints among the crosses on the graves, did not leap over the cemetery walls, on this long night. *Virgin of all virgins blest! Listen to my fond request: let me share thy grief divine; let me, to my latest breath, in my body bear the death of that dying Son of thine.*

Katharina was afraid that Jonathan, his suit smeared with grave dirt, would burrow about screaming in the cemetery waste heap and pick out the wilted roses and carnations to offer to passing cars, or else carry them to the Drava's banks & scatter them on the gravel of the piers, and venture too close to the water. On the first anniversary of his death, she recounted, & not only to her nearest kin, she had seen a boy with a long burning candle sitting down in front of Hell. On the back side of the calvary, two blood-spattered white angels' wings dangled from a coat hanger. When I got up and dressed myself, and went up the village street with an empty coat hanger, the angels' wings had disappeared, nor were they hanging over the devil's red wings, they had vanished, and there wasn't a single feather to be found. It was a blond angel who used to lead him often over the bridge, his hair was parted to one side, he had one green eye and one blue. His wings were pink. On his feet he wore brown leather sandals, tied with a golden hair taken from the head of the devil in the calvary. Like quills dripping black ink, spruces stand on the shore of the murmuring stream. Lead me with your hand… Later, the blond boy with the pink wings spotted other children & led them off to their heavenly fatherland. *Let me lament with thee truly, and accompany thee into death. I want to mount the cross in thy praise, until my final breath.*

Katharina was afraid that her son would walk past his parents' house after the resurrection, kneel before the calvary, and join his hands, with their twenty-centimeter-long, spiraling fingernails, which had continued growing under the earth, and would call, not to his mother, nor to his earthly father and siblings, but to the Godless one, the Fallen Angel, and would free him from Hell on Saint Nicholas' day. She was afraid that afterward, he would return to the scene of the disaster in his suit smeared with grave dirt, a plastic rose in his buttonhole, climb back onto the beam and jump; though maybe he would hesitate, waiting for Leopold, who was buried in the Protestant cemetery four kilometers from the Catholic one, and might still be ambling down the highway, or in the damp Ponta forest jumping from one clump of grass to another, picking a bouquet of snowdrops for friends & foes and offering them to the cars with German license plates that passed by, until at last, a half-hour late, he would arrive with the flowers to the scene of the disaster, in the barn of the parish house, and they would smoke one more cigarette and roll naked in the hay until, one behind the other, with the three meter rope in their hands, grasping the rungs of the ladder, they would climb up to the crossbeam and embrace, pressing their naked bodies together, biting each other's lips until they bled and finally climbing down the ladder & making love until dawn, when the two peacocks' morning cries would rouse the village.

But Jonathan might wander with a funeral lantern through the riverside forest & paint crosses in chalk on the trunks of the alders, which the farm people cut down shortly before Corpus Christi and stand along the village road for the pastor to walk between, his monstrance raised high, with the cervical vertebra of the Catholic suicide in its lunette, as he crosses the village from altar to altar. Early in the morning, on Corpus Christi, the housewives raise altars in front of their homes or at the crossroads, with the religious paintings that hang over their beds, beneath which their children were conceived, decorating them with flowers from their gardens, bobbin lace cloths, and lit candles. Or perhaps he will set fire to his tomb, so that it blazes through the night, fed by the fires of purgatory or the sanctuary lamp in the church, and will stand before it — with a cut-glass Easter lamb holding the banner of the resurrection in his hands — just as he stood before the Easter bonfire in his red acolyte's tunic, and he and Leopold stirred the ashes with a stick, and the sparks flew & the fire crackled. A parish barn was his death chamber, the hay his deathbed. The traces were quickly wiped away. The wind that blew between the cracks in the boards dried their tears, their urine, and their sperm. They were inseparable, the townspeople used to say, before their death. In death they were separable. One was laid to rest in the Catholic cemetery, the other in the Protestant, at different hours, so the parents wouldn't have to attend their sons' funerals alone, though neither family was to be seen at the gravesite of the other. The sculptor of death masks pressed Leopold's fragile porcelain mask onto Jonathan's face before the coffin lid was screwed to the underside, and Leopold was buried in Jonathan's death mask.

My duty is to take the cross, rejoicing in his wounds. These flames of love shall safeguard me when they take me to my tomb. My Holy Mother shall speak for me, and my soul will not be doomed. Until the lenses of the binoculars were sooty and went black before her eyes, his mother Katharina stayed, gasping for air, at the open window. The birch leaves crackled softly. Two or three ravens, posted on power lines, cawed and shook their wet wings. She heard the flick of horses' reigns as they passed the forest's edge. The playing of an organ grew ever dimmer. The interior of his coffin had been inlaid with a birch veneer. Not above the clouds, mingling over the village, but in the soot-black vault of the calvary, she heard a fierce storm, and saw lightning bolts crisscrossing over the profaner of Christ, who wrestled with the fallen angel on the floor, and heard the growl of thunder and the lash of rain against the hissing flames. But I held onto his gallstones in the Sirius matchbox! The wet skeletons of two young hedgehogs still lay on the floor of Hell. The hands of the blond angel, wading pink-winged through a running stream, were bound together by the rope with which the two boys found their release.

Savior of the world! Heed the word of thy humble servant. Come into the shell of my flesh... Satan, stretching his head from the calvary, tried repeatedly to snatch the mourning veil from the face of a widow trailing a coffin, but only grasped at air.

Her son's tomb, floating & trembling over the other graves, looked again for its abandoned hole in the earth. Jonathan bowed his head and brought his hands together, their nails grown into spirals, in prayer. Katharina closed the window, wiped her fingerprints from the lenses of the binoculars, stumbled toward the religious painting under which, years before, her now dead son had been conceived, and lay in bed beside her sleeping husband. The mouth of her husband, the father of her son, was half-open, his breast heaved and sank. His breathing was regular. His hands, with their badly trimmed nails, lay over the white sheet embroidered with lily of the valley. A dried drop of blood clung to his left inner ear. A few gray hairs emerged from his nostrils, trembling with his breaths. On his neck, to the right of his Adam's apple, a mole sprouted curly hairs. Never in his life had he dared to cut the hairs on that mole. A gust of wind rattled the casement, the quivering spider webs awoke their captive insects, which went back to struggling for a moment before falling still. The shepherd, framed in gold leaf, herding his sheep, shattered his crook and tore open his stomach over the sleeping couple, spilling gray, bloody entrails from his wound onto the double bed, in which the screaming Katharina, with eyes wide open and curly hairs on end, peered at the dark cross in the windowpane. She touched the scars on her flat torso, her damp armpits, saw with her closed eyes, shrouded but still clear, floating back and forth on the inner side of her eyelids, her breasts, which the surgeons had disposed of in a sterile bag years before. Pointing at the scars that had healed over my chest, they asked me if I wanted to see a plastic surgeon, and I said it wasn't worth it. I still have my own teeth anyway, minus two or three, and my eyes are as good as ever. Katharina felt for the glass of holy water — a few drops fell on the pink rosary from Lourdes — let her head sink in the pillow, pulled herself deeper into the bedspread, & breathed in the scent of her own body. The restless casement had in the meantime grown still, and the rustling of the green birch leaves was softer. Between the cracks in the stone cemetery walls slept the brown and green lizards that ran up and down the ancient sparse ivy tendrils growing on the ossuary walls. Hidden behind the elder bushes, the children used to point their slingshots at the lizards' heads. How often he would bring lizards' tails back to the house. Get out, I would say to him, throw it away! A column of smoke, thinner and ever thinner, rose from the tomb and dissipated. Over the blackened, curved wick of the candle she saw a shimmering rainbow. The crooked crucifixes, rusty and broken, righted themselves over the grave mounds and threw holy water on one another. The falling hosts, white and spinning on their axes in the air, imprinted with the verso of a sheet of blotting paper on which a tomb floating over a graveyard is drawn, land in the snow beneath a gray angel's wing still hovering in the air. Held tight by two young boys, two accordions, slashing their lungs, fall over the high wall of the cemetery, swinging back and forth against its cold surface.

While Jonathan lay on his deathbed in his parents' house, his bluish red rope burns and strangulation bruises covered with a fresh garland of carnations, purple and aromatic, from the garden, and his corpse had turned wax-yellow and his fingernails blue, his mother, in a black dress, kept vigil through the night, near the two candles that lit up his face to the left and right of the sofa, never once closing her eyes. Over and over she begged him to open his eyes, to rise up and to leave her forever, to go off with his guitar to St. Pauli on the sea if he wanted, but to live, to live, to be alive again. At three in the morning, as the pendulum clock struck, she beat the dead boy's chest, crying and screaming, with her ringed hand — a golden relic of her matrimony — & cried: Jonathan, stand up, I'm telling you, stand up! From the two thick funeral candles, burning to the left and right of the sofa, she gathered the streaming wax, molded it into two small crosses, and sewed the small, pliant crucifixes into the seams of his blue funeral suit.

Early in the morning, the undertakers came and pulled the corpse from her quivering, tear-dampened hands, wax-flecked and redolent of wax. Her husband, who wished to be spared the spectacle, stood in the stable between two brown and white spotted cows, wailing aloud — Boy, why did you do this to us! — his hand grasping one of their horns, & rested his forehead on the swollen ribcage of a pregnant cow. The older sister and younger brother of the deceased were curled up in a fetal position — the little one pressed his kneecaps into the knee-hollows of his sister — in the bedroom in the bed of the deceased. The crucifix in the kitchen descended from the holy corner and hid behind the slowly but steadily shrinking funeral candles, before falling, like a high-jumper, onto its back atop the coffin, where it was nailed down. Weak-kneed, ironing out the wrinkles in the coverlet with her hand, his mother bent down over the empty sofa. Her gray hair was disheveled, her lower lip exposed a few teeth, her sunken cheeks had a bluish sheen, and her heart beat louder than the striking of the woodpecker against the bark of the tree trunk not far from the window. In the furrows in her forehead, grown deeper in the course of the night, her racked and tattered soul was interred, swathed in its grave clothes & embalmed by the young soul of Jonathan, which departed his body after a hemp rope had broken his neck, under the beam and over the wood floor. The corpse-lackeys grabbed his lifeless body by the shoulders and legs — in the end, his mother was present — laid him gingerly in the coffin, and covered him up with a piece of wood, painted black, with the crucifix from the kitchen nailed to its lid. She wanted her son to lie exposed in the house of his birth, but the sanitary code in Carinthia dictates that the dead may not lie exposed for viewing for three days in the houses, that they must instead be brought to a public morgue prior to the burial. In special cases certificates of exemption are granted, but until one receives notice from the authorities through official channels, be it good or bad... In the end, the two blue coffins of the young suicides stood beside each other in the mortuary in Großbotenfeld on two catafalques resting on rubber wheels. No troublemaker switched the death notices or left a plastic fire truck near the glass of holy water holding a spruce twig, no, nothing was changed, everything was bitterly serious, and the condolences, for the most part, were dry as bone. With flecks of dry wax on their shined shoes, this person or that walked out of the chapel, crossing themselves or pressing a handkerchief into their nose, eyes, or mouth. After her death — Jonathan's mother Katharina died of cancer of the breast — she was laid in her son's tomb. The gravestone that had marked Jonathan's tomb for more than fifteen years was changed, and in its place was put a larger stone engraved with the names of the boy and his mother. *This his cross is my salvation, this his blood abides in me.*

Jesus died on the cross for me, I am his heir in eternity.
Mother, when my time comes to die, I beg thee, stay by me.

THE SUCCESSOR TO THE PAINTER OF HELL, the pastor Nikolaus Nußbaumer, often trotted out his trained dog before the acolytes; when he made a sign, it would adopt an attack pose in the backseat of his car, open its jaws, with their lips leaking spittle, and show its crooked, wax-yellow teeth to the children who watched it through the windshield; and when he gave another sign it would curl up, meek as a lamb — so that I may in Heaven come — and take its place in the back seat; since the time he ordered the house of the former sacristan across from the cemetery destroyed, the barn where Roman hanged himself is the building closest to the cemetery on the right hand side of the village built in the form of a cross, and Jonathan's parents' house is the closest on the left. The two houses of the dead and the cemetery have come together.

The church keeper Johanna Jessernig lived for decades in the sacristan's house. She grew flowers in her garden beside the cemetery wall and placed them in vases on the high altar and bye-altars, dusted the figurines of the saints, cleaned the floors of the church weekly, and, during the sacrifice of the holy mass, sat praying in her pew, not far from the black confessional. Shortly after the death of Balthasar Kranabeter, the pastor and painter of Hell, she drew people's attention by her ever-stranger speech, she no longer recognized many of the people from the village, she mixed up the children, and would go several times a day with the empty milk can to the farmer to ask whether or not she had picked up the day's milk. At Jonathan's burial, she was seen by the townspeople kneeling and praying out loud before the calvary. Fanning herself with a kerchief and striking it against the painting, she dusted off the fires on the floor of Hell & the devil's unfurled glowing wings, and repeated: What is a suicide doing in our cemetery? At her feet, her brown milk can rested atop the flattened snapdragons. She never missed religious service for decades, whether at six in the morning in winter or in the middle of the night. She was presented to the dean and the vicar general, shook the hand of the bishop of Gurk, who gave her his blessing; she could be found at the church at every baptism, wedding, and funeral; still, Johanna Jessernig refused to go to Jonathan's burial, preferring to lend her services to the poor sinner in Hell. After her death — she was buried just a few meters from the suicide Jonathan Steinhart — the pastor Nikolaus Nußbaumer, who never took his trained dog into the cemetery or the sacristy, instead leaving him shut up in his car at the cemetery gate, had the sacristan's filthy house knocked down, along with the barn and the ossuary. To make way for the expansion of the cemetery, he also had cleared the two fruit and vegetable gardens bordering the old cemetery wall — one belonged to Maximilian's mother, the other to Johanna Jessernig. All the farmers in the village seem to have contributed with diligence to this development. *Toi qui, pour consoler l'homme frêle qui souffre, Nous appris à mêler le salpêtre et le soufre, Ô Satan, prends pitié de ma longue misère!*

IN THE MIDST OF A FEUD, not long before the double suicide of Jonathan & Leopold, the sacristan Gottfried Steinhart screamed at his son-in-law, Kajetan Felsberger, in his yard over a rotting fence held together with rusty nails: I hope you drop off like the Kohlweiß innkeeper! The owner of the Kohlweiß inn was run over & killed by a bus, blindsided as he passed on his bicycle through a narrow and curvy thoroughfare in the Lieser valley — to one side was the roiling river, to the other the damp stone wall, steep and dripping water. A bus coming around the curve caught him in its yellow jaws, rolled over the bicycle, and sent the Kohlweiß innkeeper flying with a broken neck over the guardrail and down into the river's rapids.

Jonathan's grandfather, a bald man, very tall, served the people and the church as sacristan for decades. He was the only one in the village who knew how to bang the keys on the organ and could play along to the Sunday hymns. Three times a day he pulled the rope of the church bell — he tolled the big bell, the feebleminded

Oswin the small one — prepared the chasuble for the pastor, helped him to get dressed, lit the meter-long candles on the altar before Mass and snuffed them out when the services were over, and took care that there was enough Samos wine in the sacristy, as it would be converted into the blood of Christ during mass and the priest would drink it from a golden chalice that rested on the tabernacle. The pastor Balthasar Kranabeter, painter of prayer cards & images of Hell, never washed out the golden chalice with water, he always wiped it off with a freshly ironed white cloth. When someone in the village died, the sacristan went into the sacristy, tolled the bells, and, in the winter snow as well as in the summer heat, when all around the chirping of crickets could be heard, led the funeral train with a polished crucifix on a wooden staff, raised high over the heads of the mourners, glimmering gold in the sun. When the sacristan was sick, the organ would go mute, but the toothless little halfwit Oswin, wheezing heavily, especially in winter, when his breath would burst visibly from his mouth, would lead the procession with the crucifix, toll the bell with the acolytes, & perform the other offices of the sacristan. The church wives would press in together and cling to one another's sleeves as not to slip on the gleaming ice with the funeral wreaths they carried on their shoulders & fall under the horse sleigh bearing the coffin, or else get caught up and trampled under the frantic black legs of the horses. The farmers behind the wagon felt safer in their hobnailed Goiserer boots, they chatted about the constantly fluctuating prices of beef & pork and the unprofitable export of wood to neighboring Italy. When the casket, holding a wax-yellow young man, child, or adult in repose, was carried by the pallbearers to the final church service, the scent of the withering carnations & roses would blend with the fragrance of the figurines of saints, treated with beeswax & sprinkled with rose water, the scent of the burning wax candles, the aroma of incense and the scent of the rotting body that lay in its shoddily screwed-together coffin.

The children and adolescents were brought to their graves silently, in blue or white coffins. The adults, when their war decorations and service medals could be pinned to their suits, were carried in black coffins to their final resting place by blue-suited firemen to the accompaniment of funeral marches. For the obsequies of distinguished landowners, the already maturing Pulsnitz boy's choir sang in contra tenor, with crocodile's tongues: Take me out over the Onga! The women, to whose grave clothes neither military decorations nor service medals could be pinned, and who could not be carried before their coffins on a purple velvet-covered cushion, were buried, like the children & adolescents, quietly & discreetly, but at least one person from each house would stand by the body, as they always reminded one another proudly at the funeral receptions, with beer foam on their lips and orange goulash sauce in the corners of their mouth. With an aspergil from the copper dish that lay on the shoveled-up mound of earth, the mourners would sprinkle holy water in the open grave, and with a small pointed shovel stuck in the mound of earth, they would scatter sticky clumps of cemetery dirt, which clattered on the lid of the coffin, and then shake hands with the next of kin & whisper, dewy-eyed and in a choked voice: My condolences! You're supposed to say my deepest sympathies! the pastor Balthasar Kranabeter shouted many times down from the pulpit, but the townspeople stubbornly persisted with the locution. My condolences! they went back to whispering to one another, when the black-clothed priest and his black-clothed acolytes concluded the exequies and left the cemetery, going into the sacristy to change clothes. The word sympathy did not rise to their lips, not even before an open grave.

At six in the morning, when Maximilian, the first acolyte, would stamp through the snow-covered village street, arriving at morning mass before the pastor — the snow mounds were as high as his shoulders — he used to knock first at the house door of Jonathan's parents. In the kitchen, which often smelled of donut grease and fresh milk, the toothless sacristan would stand at a hammered tin washbasin, his torso exposed and his broad, worn-out rubber suspenders hanging crosswise over his upper legs, lathering his armpits, belly, & his nipples, which were ringed with long white hairs, with a bar of turpentine soap impressed with a stag with antlers, and he would scratch his itching shoulders, speckled with moles & liver spots, with the antlers. At times, when his daughter-in-law Katharina had just lit the stove & had fitted the five or six clattering, concentric stove plates one inside the other, the kitchen would smell of a mixture of donut grease, milk, and oven smoke.

After the daily ritual of washing with the deer soap, the sacristan & Maximilian would go to the church together and pull the bell rope in the sacristy. Not long afterward the pastor, Balthasar Kranabeter, would appear, kneeling down to pass through the door of the sacristy, and bless the early risers with the words, Praise Jesus. A few years after the suicide of his grandson Jonathan, someone else led the funeral procession, carrying the long black wooden staff with the polished gold Lord of Nazareth at the top, because the bald, toothless old organist, sacristan, and landowner, Gottfried Steinhart, who had not dropped off in the rapids like the Kohlweiß innkeeper, but had rather died naturally, a few years before his son-in-law Kajetan, lay in the lacquered black coffin, a rosary wound through his joined hands. His funeral procession did not pass by the calvary, because the sacristan's farmhouse lay near the cemetery, at the end of the village built in the form of a cross. His skeleton lies over the skeleton of his daughter-in-law, Katharina Steinhart, who at night, after the bells tolled, when all was quiet in the village, no calf lowed from hunger, no dog howled, and no rooster lifted its head with its comb raised and its neck stiff to let out two or three cries, when the peacocks had nestled into their hollow under the gangway or curled up by the warm chimney on the ridge of the rachitic farmer Hafner's roof, used to take her old Zeiss binoculars in hand — an inheritance from her father, who one day, surrounded by hunting trophies, lay on his deathbed with a curled moustache — and stare fixedly at the candlelight that flickered over the hillock beneath which her seventeen-year-old son Jonathan crumbled to dust. *Almighty God, father of heaven and earth, before you your creature kneels in the dust, to thank you for the virgin birth & the Holy Spirit that comforts us.*

THE NINETY-YEAR-OLD MAN with the gray-flecked moustache and the trimmed brows returned home agitated from a visit to his brother-in-law Kajetan, hung his filthy, worn-out hat on the red porcelain knob of the coat tree in the kitchen, and called out: That Kajetan! He's drinking black coffee again. He's got heart problems as is. Coffee is like a scourge for your heart. In the clay vessel where the pandapigl was rendered from the bones of animals, to be brushed on the horses with a crow's feather around the eyes and nostrils and on the belly, to protect them from mosquitoes and horseflies, lie, over the bones of his father-in-law, the sacristan &

organist who called out over the dilapidated wall — I hope you drop off like the Kohlweiß innkeeper! — the bones of Kajetan Felsberger, who failed to fulfill his father-in-law's wishes and be run down by a bus along the roaring river, but instead, one afternoon, snacking on speck in his farmhouse, fell dead, striking his head on the edge of the table. Undisturbed by his grandfather's death, his three-year-old blond grandchild went on soaking up drops of milk with an ink-stained sheet of blotting paper from the blue-green eyes of a pair of peacock feathers. Their reflections in the window stared down at the deceased. The purple lupines arranged under the holy corner, slurping holy water loudly, & the crosses in the windows of the mourning house writhed in pain. In the orchard, the Gravenstein apples and the perry pears fell from the trees in dread. The milk glass bulb in the kitchen swallowed the eternal light & spit out shards sharp as razorblades. In the holy corner it was deathly still. A spider, weaving & spinning around Jesus Christ's loincloth, stopped a moment before casting away its thread and crouching in a loophole to wait for whatever was to come. At the moment of death, the young man and his mother were milking the cows, spinning curds & hauling the manure from the stable. The laborer tried in vain to put out a wheelbarrow full of burning wax candles. Soon afterward, when the wife of the deceased went to the kitchen for hot water to clean out the milk buckets and wipe off, as she did every afternoon, the flames of Hell on the calvary, which lay between the schoolhouse & their home, she found the body under the kitchen table. She dropped the clanking bucket in the doorway on the kitchen floor and yelled: Kajetan! For years Kajetan had been treated with mood stabilizers & heart medications by a retired doctor who is said to have given his hundred-year-old mother Leopoldine a fatal injection in the heart years back, in the room hung with framed photos of her three sons who had fallen in the full flower of youth.

After the corpse of one of his three brothers who fell in the war had been transported from Yugoslavia to Großbotenfeld by train, Kajetan brought it back to Pulsnitz in a hay cart over the rough, unpaved country road. Before saddling the horse at his parents' home, he sank a pheasant's feather in the thick bone stock and smeared the black mass, smelling of decay, around its eyes and nostrils and on its belly. With long spruce branches, he covered up the coffin, which was set atop the cart harnessed to the horse smelling of bone stock. During the desolate journey, more than an hour long, he got stuck with the hay cart in the mud of the country road, and the horse, its bulging eyes ringed with pandapigl, could not pull the vehicle from the mud; a pair of Ukrainian field hands who had been working nearby came to help, setting down their jute bags, half full of potatoes, printed with the image of a whip and the legend Café do Brasil, and pushed the hay cart laden with the dead soldier so that the horse could pull the vehicle onto the roadside and Kajetan could carry his brother's remains back to their birthplace.

A few years before his death, accompanied by his family members, Kajetan had to carry one of his grandchildren, who died of peritonitis at only a few days old, in a little white coffin with angel's wings made of goose feathers, but without tolling bells or obsequies, in accordance with the instructions of the priest and hunting dog trainer Nikolaus Nußbaumer, to the cemetery in Pulsnitz, after the mother had refused her right to have her baby placed in the coffin of a dead stranger, as is customary in the hospital in Villach, & have it buried somewhere out in the country. The child's frail skeleton lies in the clay vessel where the putrid-smelling bone stock was rendered from the bones of slaughtered animals, to be brushed on the horses around the eyes and nostrils and on the belly, to protect them from the mosquitos & horseflies, beside the bones of the sacristan and organist, who for years led the funeral processions with a crucifix turned facing the coffin, shimmering in the sun, and who shouted over the rickety fence that separated the two estates from one another, I hope you drop off like the Kohlweiß innkeeper! to his flustered son-in-law Kajetan, who suffered from a heart condition, on his way to work. After the war, & particularly the death of his three younger brothers, Kajetan had for a long while had the thought of entering the French Foreign Legion rather than taking charge of the farm, but in the end he had no courage to leave his homeland forever and give up on his estate. The child, dead of peritonitis five days after his birth, was buried in the tomb of Kajetan's grandmother, who was also the grandmother of Maximilian's mother, who, when Maximilian asked her how she found out that her three brothers had fallen, told her son the following story. She was seventeen years old and was coming back home from the agricultural trade school, when her grandmother told her of one of the brothers' deaths with these words: Michl's coming home too, but different! Michæl was rash, they said, he entered a basement in Yugoslavia, storming past everyone else, stepped on a mine and was blown to shreds, the two other brothers lost their lives on the Russian battlefields, one near the city of Nevel. It was never precisely determined where the other had died. Somewhere deep in Russia, they always said. On a memorial certificate on which the three brothers are portrayed, the following is written: Dear Parents! Take up your cross! God's eternal wisdom has ever foreseen the cross we now give you as a precious gift from his heart. His all-knowing eyes looked upon this cross before he sent it, his divine intellect has comprehended it, his wise justice has tested it, he has warmed it with his loving mercy & weighed it in his two hands, that it be not a millimeter too long nor a milligram too heavy. And he has blessed it with his holy name, anointed it with his grace, suffused it with his compassion —

and he has looked upon you & upon your courage — and so it comes to you suddenly, as a special greeting from Heaven, like alms to you from the compassionate love of your God.

On Sundays, when the pastor used to put a host into the mouth of the young Kajetan impressed with the image of Hell, and the boy, thusly favored, would take his two thirsty horses from the stables to the well after services — the cold well water, mixed with saliva, ran over their hairy lips and down over their thin black legs, littered with fat gray warts — he would lean his back against the newly built fence over which, three decades later, the sacristan and organist Gottfried Steinhart would shout, I hope you drop off like the Kohlweiß innkeeper! and turn his head, grinning, whenever the young Silvia Steinhart, his future wife and helpmeet, would show up in the window of her parents' house and take her time arranging the curtains. Soon after, Silvia would lift up her white wedding dress, overcome the obstacle, and marry herself to the neighboring Felsberger estate, back when the fence rails that separated the two farms were not yet rotted through with green-gray mold and the fence-nails were still free from rust. Little girls bearing wreaths of daisies, who had not yet ingested many hosts, would hold up the long white wedding veil in their white, slightly baggy gloves of bobbin lace, so it didn't get snagged on the fence and torn to shreds, before the priest, in the marriage ceremony in the church, split the host in two and placed the half of the body of Christ impressed with the profaner of Christ, lying among the flames of Hell, on the tongue of the farm girl bride and the other, with Lucifer inclined over the sinner, on the tongue of her farm boy husband. *O Lord, I am not worthy, to sit down by thy side, but accept my humble entreaty, in thy kingdom to reside. Still this longing, bride of my spirit, ignore not my appeal! To welcome the Easter lamb into my soul with zeal!*

The funeral procession — Kajetan Felsberger lay in the casket — did not pass by the calvary, as the farmhouse of the deceased, like that of Jonathan's parents, was in the lower part of the village, & the calvary with the image of Hell in the center, across from the schoolhouse. A few months before his death, Kajetan stood a long time before the calvary, staring at the freshly picked catkins, which had already withered and were strewing their yellow pollen to the wind, at the Adversary's taut red, outstretched bat's wings, and at his pointed chin and nose; he stared long at the horns that slowly grew, retracted, and reappeared, like the antennæ of a snail, from Lucifer's forehead, before beginning to mumble, at first incomprehensibly, and then, walking back & forth in irritation, hurling saliva, to shout, I hope you drop off like the Kohlweiß innkeeper! until his wife Silvia overheard him, ran down the gravel path between the gardens and the village street, a bucket of bloody goose feathers in her hand, & led her husband, who knelt grimacing across from Hell, back to the farmhouse.

As has already been mentioned, the cemetery was expanded fifteen years ago by the pastor Nikolaus Nußbaumer, who used to show the acolytes his trained German shepherd, but until today only the deceased mother of Adam the third, Eva Philippitsch, has been buried in this new section of the cemetery where, some time back, the second vegetable garden of Maximilian's mother used to border the ossuary that was knocked down to make way for the expansion. The ossuary stood in the way of both the living and the dead. The bone fragments they discovered when the ossuary was demolished were ministered their last rites among the vases of rotting flowers, with frankincense and holy water, funerary wreaths, plastic roses and plastic carnations, and laid to rest among field mice and rats on the cemetery waste heap. The reverend Nikolaus Nußbaumer had the parish animal, grown big as a calf, put to sleep by a veterinarian, because the bellowing of the rheumatic German shepherd reverberating in the cold entryway of the parish house where the tall, pallid, armless Lord of Nazareth stood at the wall, his skin crumbling from his body and his withered crown of thorns hanging over his face, could at times be heard from as far away as the sea of Hell in the center of the village. The bone collector lays the skeleton of Eva Philippitsch over the skeleton of Kajetan Felsberger, who suffered a heart attack in the kitchen of his farmhouse, dropped his carving knife, struck his head against the edge of the table, and was later found dead, his nose broken & his face smeared with blood, under the table. Just after his burial, his son, the inheritor of his estate, ate the piece of carved speck with a garlic clove & onion rings. The hairy rind of speck was wrapped up in wax paper by the wife of the deceased, held together with a thick red rubber gasket from a canning jar, and placed in the big freezer in the pantry among the pork portioned out into cutlets and schnitzel. The eighty-year-old mother of Adam the Third left behind in her closet a plastic bag in which lay a devotional, a crucifix, a rosary & a paper on which, in gothic script, she conveyed to her survivors that, *when the time comes,* the contents of this little plastic bag should be laid in her coffin. *King of Heaven, blessed be thy name & thy glorious domain. What Jesus wills is our command, and soon shall be obtained.*

Adam the Third, the great Philippitsch landholder, boogeyman and demon, after thorough consultation with his confamiliars, saw to it that the tombstone of his grandfather, who had also been christened with the name Adam, disappeared from the cemetery of Pulsnitz without a trace, though Adam the Third had known his grandfather, dead since the fifties and now erased from the tombstone, even longer than his own father, who was called Adam as well and who died when Adam the Third was twelve. The tomb in the old part of the cemetery, which lay across from the war monument — long is the gilded list of the fallen — was abandoned.

The family tomb was moved to the new part of the cemetery, where the names of his father and mother were carved into a new stone, while that of his grandfather, who raised him, was omitted. On the one hand, the wagging tongues in the village conjecture that the tombs of his grandfather & father in the old part of the cemetery were abandoned so that the family could avoid the cost of a second tomb; on the other, they babble, burning red and dripping spit, that for his hypocritical dirndl-wearing housewife — the peahen! as she is known among the people in the village — who keeps getting her stiletto heels stuck in the soft asphalt in the height of summer and emits low, exquisite little death wails, the care of a second tomb was too much of a nuisance. For decades she had not neglected to sweep the dust from in front of the calvary with a bundle of wheat ears on Holy Wednesday — singing all the while — and to soothe the Adversary with the stiff, tickling, gold-colored husks, scrubbing his burning red belly. *O how splendid are the wounds suffered by God's son. The angels are rejoicing, death is overcome. Alleluia.*

Adam the Third spoke up about the undesirable newborn cats on his farm, scabrous and still blind; in other cases, he looked down on the Catholic Church and dismissed its rites with the words, Puppet Show! Farce! and nowadays he only shows his face in God's house during the holy days, for reasons of decorum: the newborn cats, those little cripples, should be wiped out. I'll hurl them to the floor or else I'll throw them against the wall of the stable, till they're done in! His son responds to the name Adam as well and has his own son, red-haired, who was christened with the name of his father, his grandfather, and his great-great grandfather, whose presence was expunged from the cemetery in Pulsnitz. Once, years back, when the now ninety-year-old man with the gray-flecked moustache and the trimmed eyebrows looked over the dilapidated fence that separated the two estates down into the carriage of the newly born and youngest Adam Philippitsch — Adam the Fifth — he called out in astonishment: He's a redhead! Whereupon the good wife, pushing the baby, and the grandmother, who dyed her red hair blond, shouted back from the other side of the decaying fence: Adam's got a red beard too! Without asking, Adam the Third tried to cut down a periwinkle bush from Maximilian's parents' garden, which borders the wall of Adam's family house, because it blocked his and his family's view from their new bathroom, and it was only because Maximilian's sister saw Adam the Third in their garden with a hatchet, ran to the door yelling, Don't cut it down! and informed her ninety-year-old father of their neighbor's intentions, so that the latter, raising his index finger, censured Adam the Third, that even half of the bush still stands. Cuttings from that periwinkle bush decorated the coffin of Maximilian's grandmother, Leopoldine Felsberger, who lost five children in the course of her life: three in the war, one just after birth, & one in infancy. Maximilian's godmother — the childless Hildegard Zitterer, you will remember — led the then three-year-old boy by the hand over the creaking wooden steps to the mourning chamber, took the child under the arms, and lifted him up over the coffin, decorated with branches from the periwinkle that Adam the Third had just tried to cut down, so that his family, while they splashed about in the bath and lathered themselves with a bar of turpentine soap impressed with the image of a fighting samurai to wash off the odor of the stable — Adam the Fourth had a successful spell as a karate fighter — would have a better view from their bathroom window onto the parish house barn in which, now almost twenty years ago, Adam the Third had cut the two sixteen-year-old apprentices Jonathan & Leopold down from the rope, before the arrival of the doctor and the mortician, of the priest and shepherd of souls, of the police & the gendarmerie, the fire brigade and the water brigade. He had to, he couldn't let them hang there any longer.

On Krampus Day, Adam the Third liked to go dressed as the boogey man, with a red mask & horns, with his sister Karoline dressed as Saint Nicholas, rattling a cowbell and passing out horse apples door to door throughout the village; he would knock on the doors with a bundle of rods, until the parents let in the two disguised siblings, and standing before the children, who had been stuck in the house since early afternoon, he would present a St. Vitus' dance, pounding the floor with a bishop's crosier, shaking his chain and beating the bundle of rods against the table while the children clasped each other & knelt under the holy corner. The frightened children cried and were showered with dry splinters. The Saint Nicholas with the cotton beard, straining to change her woman's voice to a man's, made the children join their hands and pray a parody of an Our Father to her brother Adam the Third, who grinned under his mask, saying Our Adam who art in Heaven, hallowed be thy name. The grandfather on the mother's side, who had come to his daughter's house that night to see his five grandchildren and had sat down at the kitchen table, grinned and pressed the iron tip of his cane against the sheep's pelt that covered the demon's breast, pushing him backward; Saint Nicholas gave each child a red crepe paper sack with either a bishop's head printed on it, or a Krampus with his tongue unfurled to his chest, filled with peanuts, figs, chocolate Krampuses and chocolate Saint Nicholases. To the laughing grandfather and old farmer Matthias Felsberger, Krampus passed out mounds of horse apples, wrapped in straw and sawdust, smelling of excrement, again in a red crepe paper sack. Limping on his cloven hoof, turning back around repeatedly, running back to the table, clanking the chain, cursing & beating the table with his bundle of rods, Adam the Third finally departed with his companion dressed in white, long-bearded and wearing a papier-mâché bishop's mitre, beating the cowbells and scraping the windowpanes another two or three times, tramping through the freshly fallen snow.

After the slaughter — mother & daughter took charge of the bloody work — the yellow chicken feet with the sharp talons and the damp chicken heads with their half-closed eyes were thrown out over the dung heap. When Maximilian climbed up the dung heap to pick up a few plums that had fallen from his neighbors' tree onto the piled up excrement — he didn't dare step onto the Philippitsch land to pick up the fat, ripe plums that had fallen to the ground, let alone pluck any from the branches — he tied the severed yellow chicken feet together with a cord and spun around three or four times atop the dung heap, until the cord slipped out of his hands and the yellow chicken feet flew over the plum tree and into the neighbors' yard. Of every tree of the garden thou mayest freely eat, but of the fruit of the tree which is in the midst of the garden, ye shall not eat of it. For if thou eatest thereof, thou shalt surely die! Maximilian had read in his catechism concerning the fashioning of the first man Adam, when he was still a schoolboy and would climb the dung pile from time to time, to harvest a few of Adam's fallen fruits from his father's dung pile.

Adam the Fourth, often to be seen in his red Mercedes with a blue Adidas satchel in which, besides clean underwear and black flannel handkerchiefs, he toted a bar of turpentine soap impressed with the image of a samurai, wrapped in silk paper printed with Japanese cherry blossoms, once had a blue coffin set up for his first public appearance in the Lindwurmstadt, before the mayor, who was a sports enthusiast. The muscleman stared a long time at the casket. The room held its breath. The wall bars chattered their teeth. The thick climbing ropes shivered down to their deepest fibers. In his suit, white as cherry blossoms, Adam the Fourth stepped forward, lifted his right arm slowly, gave an ear-shattering cry, and brought his hand down against the coffin fast as lightning. The boards flew left and right from his hand, amid the raucous applause of the audience, which had not known whether the coffin was actually empty.

More than twenty years ago, Adam the Third brought a claim before the municipal authorities against the then seventeen-year-old mechanic's apprentice Hansjörg Schaflechner, having seen him, once again, shooting at sparrows with an air rifle. The apprentice hid the dead sparrows on the gangway of the sacristan's barn under the red roof tiles, not far from the human bones stacked up in the ossuary. Looking for the mortal entry wounds, Maximilian would pick up one bird after the other by its feathered wings, and then tuck the blood-smeared animals with their disheveled feathers back in their graves. The apprentice's family was officially cited after the complaint and forced to pay a seven hundred-schilling fine. Nevertheless, only a few years ago, Maximilian saw the muscular, red-bearded athlete Adam in his white samurai outfit — Adam the Fourth, that is to say, who goes into his new bathroom, hidden by a periwinkle bush, softens the samurai impressed in the turpentine soap with water and then maims him beyond recognition in the bushy red hair of his armpits and his reddish pubic hair — with his air rifle walking among the trees of the orchard hung with apples & pears. From behind Maximilian's father's woodshed, he pointed the barrel at the sparrows posted in the tree branches. The boys in the village didn't shoot at the robins, the woodpeckers, or the wagtails, they only shot at sparrows, the sparrows were third-class birds and no one in the village had any sympathy for them, they should be wiped out, they do nothing but eat up the chicken feed. Sometimes crows were shot too, & then tied to posts and stood out in the fields as scarecrows. In springtime, when the crows had rotted and the March sun shone through the fog, only the skeletons of the crows and a few black bunches of feathers remained hanging from the wooden posts scattered here and there across the fields of fertile earth not far from the Drava's misty shores.

At a neighborhood meeting in the inn, three villagers from Pulsnitz, Adam the Third, the hunter Ewald Oberrauner, & Jonathan the suicide's father, served alcohol to the seventeen-year-old mechanic's apprentice Hansjörg Schaflechner, who did maintenance on the combine for the farmers after the harvest & readied it for winter, so that he couldn't make it home alone. The three farmers carried the boy, drunk on beer and schnapps, through the village street on their shoulders, down to the Schaflechner household, hauled him up the steep wooden stairs to the servant's quarters, & laid him out in bed. They did not pass by the calvary, as the Schaflechner house was in the upper part of the village & the calvary, with its picture of Hell, was in the center across from the schoolhouse, but no one doubted that Lucifer had stretched out his turtle's neck in curiosity and peeked over the edge of the calvary wall to observe the men and their doings as they approached over the hill into the village. They lit a candle, opened the grated panel of a lantern, put the candle in its socket & placed the lit lantern on the belly of the drunken apprentice stretched out on the servant's bed. Then the three jokers, thinking nothing more of him, left the servant's quarters. Chanting, hooting, and singing elegies, they stomped down the steep staircase and stumbled home. He could have been burned alive, the apprentice's mother complained, if the servant hadn't come home from the inn that night and found the woman's drunk son in his bed, the lit lantern resting on his belly.

Year after year, especially at Christmas, Adam the Fourth has himself sent a case of soaps packed in wood shavings from Japan, each bar individually wrapped in silk paper printed with Japanese cherry blossoms and sealed with a gold sticker the size of a coin; he wraps them up in wrapping paper printed with lit candles, green spruce branches, & winged, disembodied angel's heads, and lays them beside the Holy Kinship under the Christmas tree. *This is the day the Lord has made, I heartily rejoice. Today the Lord has thought of me, his praises fill my voice. Salvation from his mother's womb is also here for me. I thank her child, who rose from the tomb, & from death set me free.* Sometimes the bubbles from the soap lather threaten to choke the samurai, sometimes a red armpit hair, stuck in the soap, gets wrapped around his neck or even strangles him. When the samurai in the soap begins to wither, the red-bearded athlete, while playing with his muscles in the bathtub, preparing for a new display of strength, and blowing bubbles in his spruce-scented bubble bath, calls out to his dearly beloved wife, and has the next fellow warrior, wrapped up in silk paper printed with Japanese cherry blossoms, brought out of his treasure chest, & this samurai in turn slickens as soon as he makes contact with the water. As a god-fearing youngster, Adam, the muscleman, as they used to call him, was obsessed with cutting a rib from the devil in the calvary and burying it out in the fields. Let us make a man in our own image! the boy wrote with a red shard of brick on the calvary's whitewashed wall, emboldened by his weekly religion lessons & his catechism. Later he was seen many times in the center of town with a Swiss Army knife, but his parents, passersby, and even the teacher, who would pound ominously on the windowpane of the classroom, kept him from cutting off the fiend's horns and destroying the work of art. Stomping on the ground and mumbling to himself, the muscle-bound, redheaded Rumpelstiltskin, always disposed to push the envelope, walked several times around the calvary with the knife unfolded, before bringing the sharpened blade to his lower lip and smearing the devil's face with drops of blood. *Chaste and humble virgin, my due is to serve thee. On thee His breath descended, & our King was born from thee. Men, worship in dust! Woe to Hell and its prey! But good tidings to Adam's children, for the Lord is on his way.*

Mirko Posojilnica, native of Yugoslavia, whom the village people call the Yugo, who has lived in Pulsnitz for more than forty years and still speaks such bad German that he can hardly be understood, and has, to the present day, refused Austrian citizenship — I won't be an Austrian! I'm still a Yugoslavian! — and who moreover, one Good Friday, at the hour of Christ's crucifixion, scattered pushpins all over the altar and floors of the church in Pulsnitz, lay down upon them, and sang Great God, we love thee, we praise thy strength! stood drunk out in the street recently, crying in the blizzard and blathering to Rudolf Lamisch, the new pastor, while spittle dripped down the bulge of his blue lower lip: Mister pastor, I need my baptismal certificate, give me my baptismal certificate, they want to do away with Mirko, I'm going back to Yugoslavia, to my homeland, Mister pastor, give me my baptismal certificate! As the churchman, who had tried to calm him down, went back up the hill to the parish house with the armless, life-sized Crucified that one of his predecessors had salvaged from a stream bed, the Yugo walked crying and blathering down the village street, caked in freshly fallen snow, to the calvary, and kept whining: they want to do away with Mirko!

His wife cleans the church every week & decorates it with flowers she cuts in the village, going from garden to garden. On the Sunday services flowers from each of the Catholic houses adorn the main altar & bye-altars. Her son, so the woman recounted, ran his sled into a tree when he was fourteen and has stuttered ever since. Once, when they were in the center of town, opposite the schoolhouse where they had spent eight years together, contemplating the flaking, bleached-out flames of the calvary, which had been neglected since the death of the painting pastor, Balthasar Kranabeter, her son stammered to Maximilian: Today I have to go to slaughter again, I have to go up the mountain and slaughter a pig, I have to slaughter! As a stuttering child — passively subordinate to the first acolyte Maximilian — he had exalted the almighty Father, creator of Heaven and of Earth, at mass with the other acolytes.

From time to time, especially in spring, when the laburnum blossoms right and left around the walls of the calvary and the bees, after the winter's pause, buzz again in the beehive, his father, the Yugo, can be seen in front of the calvary, his head bowed and his hands joined — spittle dripping from his bluish lower lip — on his knees below the screaming sinner with his hands stretched up toward Father Abraham, beneath the pitiless devil and the restlessly flickering flames, praying the Our Father in his mother tongue. *Oče naš, kateri si v nebesih, posvečeno bodi tvoje ime! Pridi k nam tvoje kraljestvo! Zgodi se tvoja volja kakor v nebesih, tako na zemlji!*

RECENTLY IGNAZ UNTERBERGER'S WIFE WAS found under a blossoming apple tree after a fainting fit, her face turning blue, and taken to the hospital in Villach by the Red Cross ambulance with its blue lights & howling siren. Her husband, whom the farm people used to go to and borrow the bolt-gun, the buffer, which was stored in a hardwood box lined with fine green felt, its cartridges tucked in the hollowed-out niches, died from a heart attack more than ten years back, just hours after being admitted to the hospital — his skeleton lies in the clay vessel where the putrid-smelling bone stock was rendered from the bones of slaughtered animals, to be brushed on the horses with a crow's feather, around the eyes and nostrils and on the belly, over the skeleton of Eva Philippitsch, the birth-mother of Adam the Third. For six months after his grandmother's death, Adam the Fourth wore a black nylon band on his right arm, in his competitions at home and abroad. After his exhibitions, the tattered nylon band sometimes lay on the tatami and was taken home joyfully as a souvenir by his young male & female fans. On the damp floor of the shower there was always a wet, clumped-together piece of silk paper printed with cherry blossoms. During a half-year of mourning, the Carinthian samurai dedicated his international victories to his deceased grandmother Eva, who, fifteen years after the expansion of the cemetery, courageously elected to be the first to have herself laid to rest in the place where Maximilian and his mother used to pick white & red radishes, cut lettuce heads and, with the earth-caked kitchen knife still in their hands, carry the vegetables past the buzzing beehive under the clouded sky and the painting of Hell to their house in the upper part of the village. When the seasoned young farmer, a devotee of native Carinthian dress, was thrown to the mat by a slant-eyed foreigner, Adam the Fourth turned his back on sports & dedicated himself to the increase, enhancement, and glorification of his estate, which he had taken over quite early from Adam the Third. Adam the

Third, after transferring him the farm, was not seldom to be seen in tears as he repaired his Krampus mask or deloused the black sheep's pelt from his Krampus costume. His sole consolation was his redheaded grandson, Adam the Fifth, who drove a plastic tractor back and forth between the house and the stable, the sand pile and the planters, imitating the noise of farm machinery.

When the hardwood case lined with green felt lay open and empty on the window ledge in the kitchen in front of the flowers in their pots, the squealing pig, bucking and driving its hooves into the cement floor slick with excrement, would be pulled down the ramp of the stable with a rope. At a shaving trough filled with steaming hot water, made of wood held together with rusty iron rings, the buffer was pressed to the pig's temple. Maximilian hid in his bedroom, lay in a fetal position under the bed and held onto his sex organs. Only after it discharged did he let go of his still-hairless genitals and crawl back out from under the bed. The pig kept kicking, but could no longer make a sound when the now ninety-year-old man with the gray-flecked moustache and the trimmed brows, known near and far as the pig-gelder and called now and again to extract the testes from the young hogs, stuck a butcher's knife into the dying animal's throat and blood ran over the knife and over the back of his hand. The deaf maid, who had a rosary wrapped around her hand, held a washbasin under the wound and caught the warm foaming blood. The blood-caked rosary would stay several days on the windowsill of the smoke kitchen, until it was washed with a Hirsch turpentine soap and hung out on the balcony on the wash line between the men's and women's white underwear. Only when, with God's blessing, the morning sun's rays beamed down & dried the clean rosary did the maid take her keepsake from Lourdes down from the clothesline and place it on the nightstand in her bedroom. The old man of ninety with the trimmed eyebrows and the gray-flecked moustache never charged his son Maximilian with going to the Unterburgers' to fetch the bolt gun or to bring it back to them, he went himself, just to be safe, or sent Maximilian's brothers, whom he trusted more. Instead of money, the family from Naz, as they were called, was given a few kilos of fresh pork, a few frying sausages with gut casings, or a salami in a synthetic casing.

THE KLAGENFURT POLICE called the gentleman with the gray-flecked moustache and the trimmed eyebrows and asked him whether he were the brother of the Eduard Kirchheimer who resided in the Lindwurmplatz in Klagenfurt. It seemed the tenants in the building had not seen him for several days, a scent of rot was detectable in his entranceway, and the fire department & finally the police had been called. As the policeman revealed that his brother Eduard had died — Your brother is deceased! — Friedhelm, his younger brother, a retired schoolteacher & former SS-man, dropped in by chance. The gentleman with the gray-flecked moustache & the trimmed eyebrows asked Friedhelm whether he couldn't call Lazarus and give him the news that Eduard had died, because he, the gentleman with the gray-flecked moustache and trimmed eyebrows, owing to a dispute over the estate — fat-lobed Lazarus called him an estate-robber — had had no contact with his older brother for decades, and they only saw each other once a year, at the blessing of the tombs on All Saints' Day, where they stood staring stubbornly at the candles flickering and crackling on the graves, looking neither left or right, or at most shook hands at their parents' tomb, though without exchanging a word. That's not for me to do! The schoolteacher answered evasively. Why can't you call him and tell him Edi's dead. Didn't we all crawl out of the same hole?! the gentleman with the gray-flecked moustache and the trimmed eyebrows answered, but, wanting to avoid a fight, he dialed nonetheless. Plump little Lazarus with the fat earlobes picked up the phone. Oswald here! — So what! What do you want! — Edi's dead! — I'm sick. I've got sunburn. I did everything for Eduard, and I never got any thanks for it. The whole family can kiss my ass. Make a scene of it if you want! — Nobody's making a scene, our brother's dead! — After these words, the gentleman with the gray-flecked moustache and the trimmed eyebrows hung up the receiver without saying goodbye. He told his brother Friedhelm that he thought the telephone would explode, Lazarus had screamed at him so loud, just for notifying him of their brother's death. Today the ninety-year-old man regrets even having called. I should have just mailed him the obituary! he often says to Maximilian.

Only recently, by chance — thanks to the intervention of Lazarus' son, the brothers came to exchange a few words a year — the ninety-year-old man ran into his ninety three-year-old brother Lazarus, who also wore a gray-flecked moustache, in a field on the banks of the Drava, & asked him if he was getting along well. What else could I ask for! the ninety-three-year-old man with the fat earlobes and the gray-flecked moustache answered lapidarily, with a shrug of his shoulders. On another occasion, they spoke of their brother Friedhelm, who would soon be entering his nineties. Friedhelm is the only one of the brothers who does not wear a gray-flecked moustache. He hasn't done anything, he doesn't even own his own house, he's passed his life in a little apartment, so says Lazarus Kirchheimer. Plump little Lazarus, with the fat earlobes and the gray-flecked moustache, reserves the term *miscarriage* for those of his acquaintances who have not succeeded in their professional lives — That one's nothing but a miscarriage!

Their alcoholic brother Eduard, often to be met with in his pajamas in the center of Klagenfurt, a bottle of wine in hand, was buried in the Annabichler cemetery alongside his wife, the pastry chef, who fell dead twenty years before her husband in the Rabitsch pastry shop in the Lindwurmplatz in Klagenfurt, in front of the customers buying their Christmas cookies, who stepped back in horror and snuck out the door of the business.

IN THE CLAY VESSEL where the putrid-smelling bone stock was rendered from the bones of slaughtered animals, to be smeared on the horses with a crow's feather, around the eyes & nostrils and on the belly, to protect them from the mosquitoes and horseflies, over the skeleton of the twelve-year-old child, who at a bus stop, across from a butcher's shop — slices of ham hung out over the crunchy edge of the roll — ran carelessly into the street, lies the skeleton of the bishop's chauffeur and pastry-maker Eduard Kirchheimer, who not infrequently regaled the Bishop of Gurk and his nuns with cream horns or a *Malakoff Torte*, and the skeleton of Emilie Kaiser, who lived for many decades with her brother, Viktor Kaiser, in a cabin without electricity or water and who, on Saturdays, when the first acolyte Maximilian used to go from house to house passing out the parish bulletin and would take a seat, curious and anxious, under the holy corner of her kitchen, which smelled of potatoes & polenta, would tell him of the terrible doings of Krampus and the Habergeiß in her native village in Styria, where women and children were dragged off by the devil and left maimed and bleeding in the snow-covered spruce forest. The two siblings fed themselves on home-grown herbs from their little vegetable plot, on goats' milk and chicken, and on foraged mushrooms and fruit from the forest. For a time they got water from the well in front of the house of the gentleman with the gray-flecked hair, preferably at night as opposed to during the day. When the pious Emilie died, the crusts of filth were so thick on her legs that the two corpse-lackeys had to vomit outside her front door. Around her neck she wore a tight chain with a gold crucifix, which had grown into the oozing flesh of her breast. We didn't even wash or dress her, the young corpse-lackeys said, we slung the corpse into the coffin like a log and shoved it into the Mercedes. Her other brother, who used to beg throughout the region, was found frozen in a ditch some decades back.

Only recently, Maximilian smelled rot as he passed by the feed troughs in the stable of the ninety-year-old man with the gray-flecked moustache, and stopped, where the reek of decay was strongest, before a young bull; looking at the iron chain around its neck, he saw that it had grown straight into the animal's skin. The ninety-year-old man, who had neglected to let the chain out as the bull's neck grew, tore the metal, smelling of pus and decay, from its flesh, spread thick black anti-inflammatory beech tar over the wound, wrapped the blood-smeared chain hung with clumps of hair and smelling of animal flesh, pus, and rot, in a jute sack printed with a whip and the words Café de Guatemala, & put it back around the bull's neck. As he closed the jar — black beech tar was running over his index finger — he said that the farm people, who many times let the chain sink, not only into the skin, but deep into the flesh of the bulls' and oxen's necks, had often been reported to the police for animal cruelty by the butchers, who discovered the deep wounds in the animals' necks in the slaughterhouse; and when this happened, they had to go before the judge.

Emilie Kaiser, who had worked for a season in a household in Paris, and whom Maximilian saw reading religious books and pamphlets on his frequent visits to her cottage, had a regular seat in the church, which no one disputed her. The people of the village used to joke about the two siblings, because when you approached their cottage, even from afar, you could detect the acrid aroma of their nannies and their old billy goat. Even in the church they couldn't cover up the scent of their animals, it had penetrated into their clothes. Emilie always hated the calvary & its picture of Hell. Many times she had complained to Maximilian, who carried the parish bulletin from house to house, that she couldn't understand why the pastor Balthasar Kranabeter had painted Lucifer on the wall, why he hadn't immortalized the mother of God with the Christ child, the Good Shepherd with his herd, or Saint Christopher with the Christ child on his shoulder. She refused to put flowers under Hell's sea of fire, but two or three times a year she would tie a bundle of herbs from her garden to a shingle on the calvary's roof. She had asked her brother to light a holy candle, only a holy one, in front of Hell, if one day, when the time came, he outlived her & she were carried over the village street, behind the cross-bearer, passing by the calvary to the church for her final blessing. *Bâton des exilés, lampe des inventeurs, Confesseur des pendus et des conspirateurs, Ô Satan, prends pitié de ma longue misère!*

IN A BUS STOP IN VILLACH-ON-THE-DRAVA, the twelve-year-old Lukas asked the bus driver if there was time for him to cross the street and buy a sausage roll from the butcher. The boy threw his knapsack in his seat and scurried down the steps. Just as he was crossing the street, a car came & ran the twelve-year-old down. The child died on the spot. The day after the calamity, the family received a phone call from a flower shop stating that a bouquet of flowers was there for them to pick up. When the dead boy's father, who had to identify the child in the hospital, went to the florist's, he found a slip of paper in the bouquet on which the driver expressed his condolences to the grieving parents. In court, it was confirmed that the driver was not only speeding, but also driving recklessly.

Later, the marriage produced further offspring. Two children were born, a boy and a girl. You've got two beautiful children, what more could you want! the people say when they run into the mother with her children on the street. Those two children, the people say, have their unfortunate brother to thank for their lives. If Lukas hadn't been in the accident, those two wouldn't have had more children, so say the wagging tongues of the village behind cupped hands. When she was three years old, the daughter said to her mother: I made a cemetery from Lego blocks, I left the cemetery gate open, that way Lukas can get out! *In the wounds of this heart, my soul is still. In my hours of joy & suffering, to shout to the world is my will: praised for all time, blessed for all time, be the holiest heart of Jesus sublime.*

DURING ADVENT — the open black umbrella was white with snowflakes — Maximilian sought out the ninety-three-year-old Miss Glantschnig, who had, until recently, been able to go shopping every day and cook her own lunch, but who had lately been cared for by her daughter-in-law, Marlies, in exchange for a monthly fee. When the old woman's son was taken to the hospital in Villach with a lung inflammation for the fourth time in one month, it was not he, but the daughter-in-law who brought lunch to Miss Glantschnig in her house, mounting the creaking steps with a plate up to the old woman's apartment. One day Marlies walked slowly up to the old woman with a full plate, and when she credulously reached her hands out for the food, Marlies pushed the plate into the frightened woman's breast & shoved her backward with its hard enameled lip until she stumbled, retreating, and fell to the floor. The daughter-in-law rested the plate on the dining table, knelt before the old woman, and slapped her several times in the face. More than a decade before, Marlies' face had been disfigured in a horrible traffic accident. The surgeons could just barely patch it up. In the hospital, she was specially cared for by her mother Sofia, a midwife who had delivered babies in Maximilian's parents' bedroom. After the burial of the old Mrs. Glantschnig, who lived on the second floor, they began renovations on the house for the young family. Beside this house, a ten-year-old on a bike, his legs stretched upward, rode down the hill onto a highway concealed by a wall. The gamble cost the child his life. In the clay vessel where the putrid-smelling bone stock was rendered from the bones of slaughtered animals, his skeleton lies over the skeleton of Lukas, who carelessly crossed the street, his gaze fixed on a white-clad figure moving behind the window of the butcher's shop. The child was buried in the Pulsnitz cemetery just behind the gravestone of Maximilian's grandparents. A few days after the funeral of the unfortunate, the astonished townspeople, looking through their kitchen windows, saw two uniformed priests, flanked by two acolytes holding long burning candles, carrying the armless, life-sized Jesus, who had once been cast by a blasphemer over a waterfall, out of the chilly, domed entryway of the parish house on their shoulders and down the village street, passing by the calvary and entering the church vestibule, which had been converted into a mortuary chapel. Burnt, still slightly smoking, the angels' wings that had been fixed at the four corners of the child's coffin, made of bound-together goose feathers, lay under the leaping red flames of Hell, in a pile of white-gray ash.

A FEW DAYS BEFORE CHRISTMAS, while it snowed outside, Maximilian and his father sat snacking on speck together, drinking hot rose hip tea and homemade schnapps, & the old storyteller recounted that up there — he signaled a hill with his index finger — where you see desolate bits of wall overgrown with shrubs, once stood the home of the bone burner, who used to go from house to house through the snow-covered forest & over the frosted fields, filling his satchel up with bones, especially in winter, when the farmers slaughtered their pigs and cows. All winter he kept the bones hidden from his dog in a niche in his goat pen. In spring, with the first thaw, before the draught horses were driven over the fields hitched to plows, the bone burner would rebuild his bone furnace. He would place the bone-filled clay vessel in a hole in the ground atop glowing coals, cover it with dirt and grass, and let the bones simmer until they secreted the viscous pandapigl. Often, as a child, the ninety-year-old man said, he would go to the bone burner in summer and have him fill up a beer bottle with the thick liquid with its reek of decay. While the nag fed on oats, his father would lift him to brush the liquid inside its ears, around its eyes, on its nostrils & on its belly, with a crow's feather.

One day, when the farmers were able buy a chemical compound that repelled the insects from the draught horses but did not smell of putrefaction, & the bone burner had left his furnace behind, the fourteen-year-old cobbler's apprentice Walter Spätauf set fire to the bone burner's property. The bone burner could not save his goats from the blazing building, and they were burned alive along with his blind and deaf old dog, rheumatic and reduced to a skeleton. Burning beams like black ribs, charred to cinders, fell crackling over the collapsed bone furnace. Hot ashes swirled, thousands of sparks leapt hissing & popping into the air. The bone burner, grown frail and haggard, lit up by the brilliant flames of his burning domicile and goat pen, sat on the forest's edge, with his bundle of salvaged clothes, on the slope of the hill opposite the fire, under the wind-wracked spruce branches, shouting down into the village, You pig! You pig of a neighbor! The glowing ash pile smelled of burnt goat flesh the following day. With the belongings he'd saved and the half-burnt remains of his dead goats' bones, the bone burner retreated into the forest & was never seen again. The desolate bits of wall from the bone collector's house are grown over today with tall peppermint bushes, redolent in summer. The fourteen-year-old cobbler's apprentice Walter Spätauf succeeded in smuggling a box of Sirius matches into jail, and suffocated on the smoke and fumes from his horsehair mattress, which he set on fire in his cramped, windowless cell. Scarcely a year afterward, on All Saints' Day, before the wagging tails of the mooing cows, his mother and sister had to take down the distraught father of the fourteen-year-old pyromaniac from the dung-spattered stall door. Throughout the region, on All Saints' Day, the faithful in the churches donated long altar candles, piling them up over one another in boxes the size of a child's coffin.

NOT ONLY the cobbler's apprentice and his father, Jonathan and Leopold, Roman and his father and Leopold's brother, but also the schoolteacher Florian Leibetseder, who lived with his family on the second floor of the schoolhouse, across from the calvary, and his twenty-five-year-old son took their own lives, one in Vienna, the other in Berlin. One Christmas Eve, the teacher threw open the windows of his living room & shouted Fire! Fire! out over the calvary into the night. His wife knocked frantically at the front door of Matthias Felsberger, Maximilian's grandfather, & interrupted his two-hour-long rosary. A lit candle stood on the table, in front of the photos of his three sons fallen in the war. At that late hour, the flash of her flaming Christmas tree fell onto the calvary & lit up the naked torso of the tormented, lying among the flickering flames of Hell, as well as Satan's outspread wings and horned skull. The fresh snow on the calvary roof glittered pink, the blooming Saint Barbara branches, freshly picked, shone pink under the image of Hell. The neighbors showed up with water buckets & baskets full of sawdust and put out the blaze. A candle had fallen from a branch of the Christmas tree unobserved and had ignited a half-full box of Sirius matches lying on the table. A few burn-spots on the wood floor remained, & traces of soot on the whitewashed ceiling. All that was damaged were the chocolate spruces, which had dripped down from the Christmas tree, the chocolate chimney sweep, chocolate running from his eyes & mouth, the waning chocolate half-moon, and a chocolate four-leaf-clover, stripped of its leaves. The black soot was cleaned from the gold & silver tinsel by the teacher's wife with a solution of benzene. And on Christmas day, the schoolchildren filed before the wood cottage, admiring the charred Christmas tree. The following year, the polished tinsel hung again on the Christmas tree, lit by the first strand of electric Christmas lights that had appeared in the village.

In his retirement, Florian Leibetseder, who had taught Maximilian in his first two years of grammar school, traveled from continent to continent, and would set up slide shows for his former students and his friends & acquaintances, which often turned into tests of their memory of geography. When he discovered he was ill with malignant cancer and had only a few months to live, he wrote to a friend that the time had come to undertake his final voyage, and he swallowed an overdose of sleeping pills. His son, who had fled from the narrowness of the Drava Valley in Carinthia into the big city in hopes of starting his life afresh, came to nothing in the foreign land and put an end to his life a few years before his father, in Berlin, with a pistol. The transfer of the body was entrusted to the funeral director Sonnberger, from the neighboring village, with his black Mercedes. Over the broken star of the Mercedes, the undertaker had soldered a miniature replica of the calvary with its representation of Hell.

After the schoolteacher Florian Leibetseder had left the village and taught in a high school in Villach until his retirement, the teacher Timo Wigotschnig from lower Carinthia moved into his apartment and set up house there across from the calvary with its image of Hell. His twelve-year-old son died in an accident not even ten years later. When he was taking leave of a schoolmate at the bus stop, a van struck and killed him on the roadside. His father Timo Wigotschnig, who had taught

Maximilian more than five years in grammar school, died ten years after the accident, of osteoporosis. His bones had literally disintegrated.

Spider webs, dusted with flour, could be seen in all corners of the little grain mill on the farmstead. Big, fat spiders waited for hours in their white lairs. Maximilian often entered the mill, knelt down before the receptacle, and smelled the fresh milled flour that ran between his fingers. It was in the mill — he was ten years old at the time — that Maximilian asked his father, for the first time in his life, whether he could go to the cinema. *Winnetou I* is playing! The teacher is going with us, he wants to see the movie too, both his sons are going too. *Winnetou I* is playing, Father. Karl May, understand! Over & over, for an hour, he asked if he could go to the movies. Between his entreaties, Maximilian would walk out of the mill, go into the kitchen, look in the mirror, bare his hips in the outhouse, go back into the mill. Father! *Winnetou I* is playing, the teacher... Only after an hour — not even once had he looked his son in the eyes — did he murmur Yes! softly to the receptacle, in which aromatic flour, warm & freshly milled, piled up in the shape of a pyramid. To lead off, a short film was shown of slowly overturning cars. The teacher Timo Wigotschnig, whose bone-crumbs the tale-teller and bone-collector sprinkles in the full clay vessel over the skeleton of his predecessor, Florian Leibetseder, leaned into his neighbor & whispered to him: Maximilian, this is slow-motion!

THE NINETY-YEAR-OLD MAN with the gray-flecked moustache and the trimmed eyebrows told of his younger brother Friedhelm, in the meantime grown eighty-five years old, who served in the SS in the Second World War and even today is proud of having done so, that, as a five month old child, he caught pneumonia with a high fever, and the family doctor could do nothing else to help him and so recommended that his parents, as a last resort, break the ice in the village stream with a hatchet, soak a blanket in the ice cold water, and wrap the child up in the wet blanket. Either the child will live or he'll die regardless! the doctor said. Maximilian's grandmother Elisabeth followed the doctor's orders in desperation, sank a big blanket in the ice-clogged village creek and wrapped the five month old child in the wrung-out, cold, damp blanket. A while later, she took him back out. She noted that the fever had soon dropped, the child had survived the grave and beaten the normally deadly pneumonia — there was still no penicillin in those days.

Two decades later, the child saved by the ice-cold water became a fighter in the Second World War, a fact of which he is still proud — not a lowly soldier in the Wehrmacht, but an SS man. Immediately after the end of the Second World War, out of fear of the allies, his father took a knife and scraped the lightning bolt buttons from his coat collar & the shining death's head with the two crossed bones on the peak of his cap from the photos his son had sent him during the war, which show him in his office in Nuremburg and on furlough in Carinthia. In one of the photos, his SS-insignia are only half-covered by the naked arm of his three-year-old daughter, who embraces him. He wasn't a war criminal, he always stresses; I did nothing, I was in an office in Nuremburg, I spent the whole war seated at a desk. In two other photos, in which the soldier, in a long coat, sits beneath a linden with a circle of friends, they forgot to rub out the crossed bones, the death's head, and the lightning bolt insignia. Maximilian found a photo of his parents' house from which the flag with the swastika that hung from the attic window had likewise been scratched out. Maximilian's father always had this photo of his parents' house with the swastika flag with him, with a little prayer book that his mother Elisabeth had given him during the war. While the others played cards, I read in the prayer book. Without the Lord God, I should not have survived the war. Sometimes it was a matter of millimeters, and I would have been done for, the ninety-year-old man with the trimmed eyebrows recollected.

His brother Friedhelm goes to Pulsnitz every year for All Saints' Day & All Souls' Day with his black American car, dozens of years old but looking ever fresh and polished to a glow, to pray at the graves of his parents, now three decades dead, and to take part in the blessing of the tombs. The two brothers, after sinking a pheasant's feather in the bucket that sits below the blazing flames of Hell, full of the bone stock rendered up in a bone furnace from the bones of the dead in the town built in the form of a cross, spread the black, viscous mass, smelling of rot, around their eyes, and after having fed themselves on the devil's ears, they go with their equally senior brother-in-law Klaus, as on every All Saints' Day after the blessing of the tombs, when the priest, flanked by his acolytes, has gone from tomb to tomb with a copper aspersorium and has sprinkled holy water on the yellow and white All Saints' Day flowers and the burning wax candles with the damp, gray bristled twig, and take the vertical beam of the town built in the form of a cross to the village fountain, where, decades ago, as children, sons, and farmhands, day after day, morning and night, standing between the heads of the horses, they used to hold onto the bridles while the restless horses sank their snouts in the full water trough and, snorting and slurping, sucked water into their mouths. The young farmhand, standing between the horses' heads, would breathe in the animals' foul-smelling breath. The horses would shake their heads, so that their slaver, trailing in long threads from their black snouts, mixed with the fresh, cool spring water, landed on the child's face like cobwebs, and then the pungent, sweating horses, guided by the boys holding the bridles, would turn heavily around and stomp back to the stalls in the knee-high snow.

The three old men, who survived two world wars and are prepared for a third — Get ready, you'll see, it's already getting started. Look at Yugoslavia over yonder. One world war already sparked off there — go, after the blessing of the tombs, their eyelids blackened with the stock rendered from the bones of their dead neighbors, and the hairy rinds of the devil's ears in their mouths — *In those days, when I was twenty, I was so hungry, I would gladly have eaten the devil's ears!* — to the Kirchheimer estate, take off their coats in the kitchen, hang their hats on the red porcelain knob of the coat tree, seat themselves at the kitchen table &, within a few minutes — as every year on All Saints' Day, after the blessing of the tombs, for decades — begin to talk about the war, while the two mentally ailing women, mother and daughter, start the preparations for lunch. Under the holy corner next to a burning wax candle, a memorial to the family dead, stand four freshly plucked chrysanthemums, yellow and bushy, in a jar, blessed with holy water and incense by the pastor & his acolytes. One of the three old men at the table begins leafing through the day's open newspaper and commenting on his reading.

THE FIRST OLD MAN: *Lord, have mercy upon us! Christ, have mercy upon us! Lord, have mercy upon us! Jesus, hear us! Jesus, heed our prayers!* Take a look at our parliament, a bunch of nobodies & do-nothings, sitting around, cashing checks, they can hardly be bothered to lift a finger.

THE SECOND OLD MAN: *God, our Father in Heaven, have mercy upon us! Son of God, savior of the world, have mercy upon us! Blessed Holy Ghost, have mercy upon us!* That parliament should be eradicated. The best thing would be a robust dictatorship, not a weak one, we need a healthy dictatorship.

THE THIRD OLD MAN: *O God, ever disposed to mercy & to forgiveness, accept our most humble prayer, that thy noble benevolence may redeem us & all thy servants bound by the chain of sin!* The Turks and the Yugos should be cleared out. We should close off the borders so that rabble with their twisty moustaches can't keep sneaking in. We used to have the Italians, now we have the Russian and Rumanian mafia here too.

THE SECOND OLD MAN: *Eternal God, all-powerful, who rules over the living and the dead, showing mercy to all who, by their faith and their good works, thou seest fit to be thy servants, we humbly beg thee, on behalf of those still dwelling in the world in mortal flesh and those who, freed from this life, have already been received into the other world, that, through the intercession of the saints, they receive thy benevolent forgiveness for all their sins.* We've got work enough here. Austria can feed herself. If the citizens won't take the jobs they are offered, let them go out in the streets and beg, maybe some foreigner will walk by and share some welfare money with them. There are plenty of our countrymen that could use it.

THE THIRD OLD MAN: *Most merciful Christ, my soul's sweet savior, who has loved me throughout eternity, who from love became flesh and spilled thy precious blood, open for me the gates of Heaven.* The thirties were tough. We had high unemployment. When Hitler came, everyone had a job, and they opened back up the factory on the other bank of the Drava.

THE THIRD OLD MAN: *On the way of the cross, which my savior and redeemer paved with his bloody footsteps, I shall hasten to my Fatherland, Heaven.* Who gave Adam the Third the new roof for his hay barn? Hitler! Hitler and no one else!

THE FIRST OLD MAN: *O most holy Jesus, thy lifeless body, which thou gavest over to blows & humiliation, could only find worthy repose in thy pure mother's lap. Have I not often asked thee, with thy exalted body, to come into my heart, full of sin & impurity? O, make a new heart in me, that I may be worthy to receive thy body in the blessed sacrament at the altar.* Nowadays the mailman delivers the money to the vagrants and do-nothings in their homes, so they can just stretch out on the couch counting the bills. The layabouts have lost the will to find a job.

THE SECOND OLD MAN: *O Jesus, who will give water to my head and torrents of tears to my eyes, so that, day & night, I may cry away my sins? I pray thee that through thy bitter, bloody tears, thou concedest me the grace of penitence & my heart so repents, that abundant tears may flow from my eyes, and throughout my life I may cry away thy suffering and even more so, my sinfulness, which gave rise to it.* What was it like in our day? Seven kilometers I had to walk to school, in summer and in winter. After school, when I was ten or twelve, I herded the sheep out in the fields for the farmers, and picked blueberries by the kilo along the way. I sold the blueberries, that was my pocket money. At fifteen I had to work with the lumberjacks in the forest from four in the morning on.

THE THIRD OLD MAN: *O, with what great pain was the skin ripped off with the garments, which dried in the wounds & on the blood. The garments were torn from Jesus, that he would die poor & naked. How serenely would I die as well, if stripping off man's clothes I might strip away as well his wicked inclinations.* How nice it used to be before, at the autumn fair in Kindelbrücken, where we bought wool coats, Goiserer shoes, leather gaiters, and wide suspenders. We brought the children home cream horns & Turkish honey. And now? Every three or four stalls there's a nigger selling plastic tractors and black dolls, pistols and gingerbread hearts.

THE SECOND OLD MAN: *Empty me from myself and fill me with thy endless good. Live in me, O crucified Jesus, and remain inside me, so that I may boast that the world no longer possesses me.* They should run the profiteers out on a rail. Under Hitler there was no such thing. Butter and bread, the basics, cost the same everywhere.

THE FIRST OLD MAN: *O worthy Jesus, who will make it that I too may die from love for thee! Let me at least be dead to the world!* It's the filthy Jews' fault. Nowadays the Jews run the world from America.

THE SECOND OLD MAN: *Thou art the head, we the body, through the wonderful appointment and worthy acceptance of this holy mystery. Thou hast led us into glory, wherein we, thy body, must follow thee.* My friend, Hitler knew what to do with lawbreakers! For the hard criminals, we should bring back the death penalty. The electric chair's the only thing that will sort them out properly.

THE THIRD OLD MAN: *Burn, O Lord, our kidneys and our heart with the fire of the Holy Spirit, that we may serve thee with chaste body and please thee with pure heart.* A shot in the ass would do the trick too.

THE FIRST OLD MAN: *O God, from whom proceed holy judgments & good works, give thy servants that serenity that the world cannot give, so that our hearts may live out thy commandments and, free from fear of the enemy, live on tranquilly under thy protection.* Just imagine, in the war we had a pastor who told us to kill as many enemies as possible. A pastor said that! One of my comrades told the priest he was a Christian and was sworn to keep the Ten Commandments. Do you know what the fifth commandment is? my comrade asked the priest. Thou shalt not kill! Since that time, I don't have any respect for pantywaists. In the end, the comrade took a bullet in the head. They shot out both his eyes. In the military hospital he cried out: I want to see my family again!

THE SECOND OLD MAN: *Veronica offers to Jesus, as devotion & mercy, the veil over her head as a kerchief, so that he may dry his death-pale face, covered in spit & blood, and he leaves impressed in the veil the image of his most holy countenance. A small service, & a very great reward.* The murderers and hardened criminals should be lined up along a wall and shot. That will teach them.

THE THIRD OLD MAN: *Would that I could be a friend to Christ, though I am an enemy of the cross! O dear beloved cross, I accept thee with joy from the hand of God. Far be it from me, hereforth to esteem myself happy in whatever lies outside the cross. Through this I want the world to be crucified, that I, Jesus, may be thine.* Why should the state put up with this riffraff for decades? Who pays for them? Us with our taxes, and no one else.

THE FIRST OLD MAN: *Be constant in good and do not stray from the cross. Who perseveres to the end, shall be rewarded.* We need a little Hitler to bring back peace & quiet to the country. Someone needs to crack down.

THE THIRD OLD MAN: *O Jesus, merciful lamb! I must repent of my weakness and impatience. I curse them. Take up my flesh & crucify it with thy zeal. Cut me, burn me, torment me in this life, if thou willst, only spare me for eternity.* Hitler wasn't so bad; it's the little Hitlers that fouled everything up; that's why we lost the war.

THE FIRST OLD MAN: *Therefore I renounce the devil, the world, & the flesh and detest all infernal temptations, all the vanities of the world and sinful lusts, for now and for ever.* If Hitler hadn't gone after the Jews, we would have won the war; we would have pushed on through Stalingrad. There was no relying on Mussolini.

THE THIRD OLD MAN: *With thy holy grace, I promise thee henceforth to keep free from sin, not from fear of Hell, not from the promise of eternal glory, but from love for thee, because thou art my God, of infinite love worthy.* You can see it even today. The farmers get less & less from the Italians for their meat and wood. The Italian is almost like another Jew.

THE SECOND OLD MAN: *O Jesus, he is not worthy of thee who will not take up his cross & follow thee. I will help thee bear thy cross. I will be thy friend & companion in thy via crucis. I will step in thy bloody footprints & follow thee.* Hitler should have exterminated twice as many Jews.

THE FIRST OLD MAN: *Whoever, in this life, had no place to rest his head, has not a grave of his own in this world, because he was not of this world. You, who cling to this world, eschew it, so that you do not meet your end with it.* Take a look at all the money the chancellor has shipped off to Israel. Now the state has to care for the Jewish cemetery too.

THE SECOND OLD MAN: *Ay, sinless Jesus, I have sinned. Yet thou acceptest the judgment of death so that I may live. How am I to live, then, but for thee alone? So long as I try to please men, I cannot be thy servant. Then I will displease men & the world, so that I may please thee alone, O Jesus.* They closed down Mauthausen much too early.

Even before the water drops on their coats had dried into the green loden & the seeped-in smell of the smoking grave candles, the aroma of the yellow and white chrysanthemums on their clothes and the rotting smell of the bone stock around their eyes had mixed with the aroma of the kitchen, the scent of frying omelets and chopped onions growing stronger — as every year on All Saints' Day after the blessing of the tombs — the body of a soldier, cut in half, was picked up under the armpits by his comrades after an air raid, among the howls of those surrounding him, & placed once again on top of a waste heap, where it remained more than an hour, amid the laughter, praying, and singing of his comrades, until it tipped forward & the soldier's face, blood-smeared and streaked with soot, already blue with rigor mortis, landed in the mass of rotting food scraps. Beside the bisected corpse, lying with its face in the waste heap — as it had been for decades on All Saints' Day, after the blessing of the tombs — a soldier again had his head shaved for having stolen from his comrades, was stripped naked and tied to a stake for twelve hours under the pouring rain beside the waste heap, near where his compatriot lay with his body ripped in half. Around his neck hung a placard that read: I robbed my fellow soldiers! The mentally ailing daughter of the ninety-year-old man with trimmed eyebrows, his eyes surrounded by black bone stock, licking his red and hairy devil's ear, laid the countless bloody pork chops that had been thawed out the night before All Saints' Day on a cutting board and beat them with a wooden mallet, its striking face covered by a serrated iron plate. The mute, mentally ailing wife of the ninety-year-old man — who had lost three brothers, cut down in the full flower of youth, in the Second World War — was slicing thin strips of frittata as long as plates on a cutting board, and heard in the background, intermitted by the blows of her daughter's mallet against the pork chops — as every year on All Saints' Day, after the blessing of the tombs — coming from the mouth framed by the gray moustache, in a familiar voice, that during the buildup to the war — Just try and imagine it! — a Panzer rolled over a hole in the ground where a man was huddling; the Panzer spun left and right several times over the hole in the ground, but the narrator, whose head and shoulders were covered with dirt, stretched his head out and was able to crawl from the tomb alive. From the holy corner, decorated with All Saints' Day flowers, where the three old men sat, gnawing & slurping on the hairy rinds of the Devil's ears, staring attentively at each other's faces, their eyes ringed in black, the mute woman, seventy years old, heard in the background, while she cut the thin, plate-length strips of frittata on the wooden cutting board — every year on All Saints' Day, after the blessing of the tombs, the same lunch was prepared — intermitted again and again by her daughter's mallet blows against the pork chops, that over another hole in the ground, inside which a soldier huddled, a Panzer skidded likewise back and forth, so that the earth crumbled over the head and shoulders of the soldier; but this time the supple earth gave way and the tank dropped down in the hole and crushed the soldier. While the seventy-year-old farm-wife cut the next plate-length frittata into thin strips, her daughter laid the next bloody piece of pork on the wooden cutting board and struck it with short, precise blows, so that the blood drained from the crushed meat into the grain of the wood, & the war correspondent shouted louder, gazing alternately at the white aprons of the two women preparing the midday meal & the faces of the two other old men gnawing on the hairy red devil's ears amid the ever-louder hammering of the mallet: He was squashed like a mouse, like a mouse, imagine, and that was just in the buildup to the war and not in the war itself, like a mouse... The drops of holy water had in the meantime soaked into the coats of the gentlemen war correspondents and the drops of wax on the green loden, hardened by the cold of the graveyard, slowly softened in the warm, humid kitchen, smelling of bone-stock and candle wax, All Saints' Day flowers and simmering cow's bones. The daughter of the ninety-year-old man of the house cracked an egg against the hard edge of a white enamel bowl, spilled the white from the two halves of the eggshell, brown and serrated, in the first enamel bowl & the yokes in another, laid the pounded pork in the bowl with the yellow egg yolks, which she had beaten with a fork, and breaded the meat in a third enamel bowl filled with bread crumbs. The breaded schnitzel was laid in the loudly crackling lard, already heating in the pan, and its scent mixed with that of the bone stock that the three gentlemen would smear around their eyes in front of the calvary in the middle of town on All Saints' Day, just after the blessing of the tombs, with the words, *Beloved Jesus, in thy travails, I wait to anoint & succor thee.* After the seventy-year-old farmwife had cut all the frittata, she opened the oven door and placed one knotty spruce branch after another on the fire, while in the background, in front of the kitchen windows already steamed over by the boiling stock of cow bones, the three bald-headed old men, telling war stories, were pulling their chairs closer and closer together, leaning their heads in, as if each wanted to suck the trench dirt & the blood of comrades from the damp, gray-flecked moustache of the other, or lick from his companions' eyes the black bone stock, smelling of rot, which was rendered from the bones of the town's dead, or as if they wanted, like fighting dogs, to tear a morsel from the others' mouths, to suck, chew, or savor an especially succulent bite of the hairy red devil's ear — ... *I was so hungry, I would gladly have eaten the devil's ears.* One of the bald-headed war correspondents told his two attentive listeners that, in a work camp in Siberia, his long-dead brother-in-law, Willibald Zitterer, and his comrades had to drag the bodies of prisoners, worked to death, from a coal mine, but they couldn't bury them, because it was deep winter and the ground was frozen through — it was forty degrees below zero — and they had to stack the frozen dead like firewood, one on top of another, in an outbuilding, so that in spring, when the temperature rose, they could bury them in a mass grave. Not far from the labor camp stood an outbuilding, in which more than a hundred dead, frozen stiff — like firewood! the old man repeated, pulling the slimy devil's ear from his mouth — lay side by side and piled up. The old man, who used for a third time the word *firewood* to describe the frozen corpses of the prisoners stacked up one over the other, all the while striking the hairy pink devil's ear against the table in indignation, pulled his chair aside as his wife opened the drawer and dropped the knives, spoons, and forks on the table with a clang, in such a way that the tines of the forks became entangled and one of the old men — the long hairs of the devil's ear hung over his lower lip like sloppily extracted sutures — in a higher voice, because of the noise of the clanging silverware, informed his old listeners, their mouths half-open and their heads pressed together, that not far from their position, a pastor cowered in a church tower, giving up information to the English, who flew over their position and firebombed it. It must have been the Dutch who made them aware of the treacherous priest. It was nighttime, according to the old farmer with the wide-open eyes circled with black bone stock, when we aimed the barrel of the cannon at the church tower, two kilometers away. First we launched a flare to get it in our sights, and then we fired on it. The tower fell over like a blade of straw, and the priest was done for, he didn't even have time to say an Our Father, so the grinning old man told his two listeners gnawing on their devil's ears. He took a ladle of frittata soup from the steaming enamel bowl, stirred the hot soup, swimming with grease bubbles from the boiled cow bones, with a spoon, and, arching his eyebrows, told his two listeners, who kept dipping their spoons in the frittata soup & lifting them to their lips — the appetizers, pink and hairy, lay sucked dry on the table in front of their plates — that he had once taken a train home and seen the burning cathedral in Cologne, after it had been hit with incendiary bombs. From the train, he had seen people trying to flee in the streets, but they had gotten stuck in the searing hot asphalt not far from the cathedral and had been slowly burned alive. The mute, seventy-year-old wife of the ninety-year-old man with the gray-flecked moustache and the trimmed eyebrows collected the spent pink devil's ears of the three gourmand war correspondents with her bare hands, turned away from the holy corner and the All Saints' Day flowers and walked over to the stove. She opened the chrome oven door and threw the devil's ears, gnawed and sucked clean, into the leaping flames. The two mentally ailing women — mother and daughter

— arranging the chairs and sitting down at the lunch table with the three old men spooning their frittata soup and nodding with wide-open eyes, began slowly to slice and eat the devils' tongue, almost raw beneath its crust of breading. On the blade of the knife and on the white enamel bowl, thin as a thread, stretched the blood trail of the devil incarnate. *Père adoptif de ceux qu'en sa noire colère, Du paradis terrestre a chassés, Dieu le Père, Ô Satan, prends pitié de ma longue misère!*

On Christmas eve, before midnight mass, the ninety-year-old man placed a small spruce tree that his daughter had decorated with tinsel & red wax candles in the snow hill on his parents' grave, and after services, where he had sung Oh Come Little Children, Come One and All ... and Silent Night! Holy Night! with the Pulsnitz choir, he stood before the little Christmas tree decorated with tinsel and burning candles on his parents' grave, praying an Our Father and leering at Hubert Steinhart, who was visiting the grave of his son Jonathan, who had hanged himself, and on whose snow-covered grave mound there also stood a little Christmas tree, decorated likewise with tinsel & burning candles. After the ninety-year-old man, interrupting his prayers — ... blessed art thou, among all other women, and blessed is Jesus, the fruit of thy womb ... — cursed, between the lines of the prayer, the Steinhart clan, with whom he hadn't exchanged a word for decades, he blew out, one after the other, the red candles on the little spruce tree, breathing in the ever more acrid fumes. The white-gray candle smoke wound upward through the branches of the little Christmas tree hung in silver tinsel, grazed the engraved and gilded names of his parents on the gravestone, and dispersed among the meter-high iron crosses in the graveyard. The shy Hubert Steinhart, who avoided all the people in the village and was last to enter the church and first to leave, before the mass had even ended, with the spit-damp host still between his tongue and palate, so as not to bump into anyone, crouched before the grave of his son Jonathan, pulled a tangle of white angel's hair from a branch, unknotted it, and distributed the white strands clinging to his fingers among the various branches of the glowing little spruce tree. When the farmer Steinhart, with tinsel still sticking between his fingers, stood up from his son's grave, you could hear the soft cracking of his bones. After the ninety-year-old man, glancing around in irritation at the noise, had taken leave of his progenitor, who had lain now thirty years beneath the earth, whispering Bye, Pop! — with the dust of his mother's bones he spoke not a single word — and left the creaking cemetery gate behind him, he walked, as the organ notes of Silent Night, Holy Night rang out in his ears, down the village street, past the Saint Barbara branches blossoming before the flames of Hell, so that the Devil, undecided as to whether to choke himself to death or finish himself off with his razor-sharp fingernails, paused a moment and took his place again with a cup of gall over the profaner of Christ laid out on Hell's floor; he tramped by the village fountain, full of meter-long icicles, which hung over the ice-covered stream running quietly below — the sheet of ice dampened the sloshing of the stream — and the racket of war mixed with the ringing of the organ and the crunch of his hobnailed boots pressing down on the cotton-soft snow. Walking forward, he saw before him, as he looked down at the tips of his snow-covered boots, the eighteen-year-old stretcher-bearer from the trenches, who tried to staunch a graze wound in his neck and told him to get down, that for God's sakes he wouldn't attend to him on foot, but who, before he could implore him a second time, Get down! tumbled, struck by a muffled bullet from a silencer. The bullet penetrated under the steel helmet wrapped with a Red Cross bandage, through his neck & into his head. The young stretcher-bearer fell dead, his head spurting blood, into his arms. Streams of blood ran down the dead man's face. Get down! Get down! the ninety-year-old man with the gray-flecked moustache and the trimmed eyebrows murmured softly, with the organ playing the Christmas carol A Spotless Rose is Growing, From a Tender Root … still in his ears, as he passed by the village fountain overhung with icicles, stamping through the deep snow to his ancestral home, where he scattered a few grains of aromatic incense on the griddle; they immediately began smoking, & he rubbed together his thick, chapped fingers, frozen from the cold, over the range, then turned his head and looked into the faces of his family members, one after the other, as they entered the warm kitchen, returning from midnight mass. *Gloire et louange à toi, Satan, dans les hauteurs, Du Ciel, où tu régnas, et dans les profondeurs, De l'Enfer, où, vaincu, tu rêves en silence! Fais que mon âme un jour, sous l'Arbre de Science, Près de toi se repose, à l'heure où sur ton front, Comme un Temple nouveau ses rameaux s'épandront!*

HIS LORD & MASTER with the gray-flecked moustache and the trimmed eyebrows, who only shows his face in church a few times a year, on the high holy days, was pressed upon by his family members and by the pastor Rudolf Lamisch to take part in the Sunday services when the newly built mortuary chapel was to be consecrated. You have to go to the blessing of the mortuary chapel! You're the oldest man in the village! After the services, while the priest, flanked by his acolytes, carting the silver censer and the copper vessel with the aspergil, walked with his flock from the church into the mortuary chapel and began the ceremony of the benediction, splashing holy water on the floor, on the walls, and on the armless Jesus, who had been moved from the entryway to the parish house and hung on the wall of the new mortuary chapel and who had once been thrown by a blasphemer over a waterfall, to be rescued from the stream bed by the pastor & painter of prayer cards, who immortalized the sinner in his painting of Hell, the ninety-year-old man, along with the other attendees, filed into the newly built funeral hall. But I was in the very back, behind everyone else, the ninety-year-old man told his son Maximilian with a wry grin. I don't have to be the first everywhere & in everything. More than fifteen years ago he said to Maximilian: Let me just live ten more years, then Hell will be all full and I'll go up to heaven!

It was decades ago — in the days when Maximilian the acolyte used to fold his child's hands in prayer on the altar steps — that the ninety-year-old man first expressed to the painter and pastor Balthasar Kranabeter the wish that the big, unused vestibule in the church be converted into a mortuary chapel, so that the dead would need not be taken to neighboring Großbotenfeld, but could lie exposed in their native village. It long fell on deaf ears, and then another priest well-disposed to the idea met with official resistance, because the proper sanitary facilities could not be installed; but the people can go to the toilet at home, the old man said, the houses in the village aren't far from the church nor from the graveyard. At night, he declared, the mortuary chapel should be closed, because in Carinthia, not many years back, only a few days before Christmas, a dead man and his coffin were stolen by a group of men & thrown into the river. The floating coffin with the dead man was five kilometers downstream before it got trapped in among the ice floes near the shores of the Drava and had to be salvaged from the frozen river.

The people of the village want a woodwright to restore the handicapped Christ hanging in the new mortuary chapel, once rescued, soaking wet, from a stream bed; to have arms glued to his torso, so that, when the time comes, he can grab hold of the deceased and drag him off over the sea of flames, over the devil's sharp horns and his outstretched wings, billowed by the hot winds of Hell, and speed him on to his heavenly fatherland. *Our sacrifice is done, great God our father dear, we thank thee, that thou hast bestowed thy grace on thy flock gathered here.*

"To access the cells of the hermits [of Mount Athos], one must sometimes skirt abysses and climb staircases carved in rock; the sky and the emptiness, that is all there is. There may have been monks who took a wrong step and disappeared forever in the blue depths of the sea, a hundred feet below. When an anchorite dies — after a rather long time not coming to retrieve the food that is left for him — another monk replaces him; he enters into solitude, & pushes the bones of his predecessor into a corner of the hovel he will live in."

NOTE: The citation on page 3 is from Jean Genet, "L'étrange mot..." in *Oeuvres complètes: Tome IV*; that on page 194 from Julien Green, *L'arc-en-ciel: Journal 1981–1984*. The French stanzas that run throughout the novel are from Charles Baudelaire, "Les Litanies de Satan," in *Les fleurs du mal*.

COLOPHON

WHEN THE TIME COMES

was typeset in InDesign.

The text and page numbers are set in *Adobe Jenson Pro.*

The titles are set in *Charlemagne.*

Book design & typesetting: Alessandro Segalini

Cover design: Alessandro Segalini

WHEN THE TIME COMES

is published by Contra Mundum Press
and printed by Lightning Source, which has received Chain of Custody certification from: The Forest Stewardship Council, The Programme for the Endorsement of Forest Certification, and The Sustainable Forestry Initiative.

CONTRA MUNDUM PRESS

Contra Mundum Press is dedicated to the value & the indispensable importance of the individual voice.

Contra Mundum Press will be publishing titles from all the fields in which the genius of the age traditionally produces the most challenging and innovative work: poetry, novels, theatre, philosophy — including philosophy of science & of mathematics — criticism, and essays.
Upcoming volumes include William Wordsworth's *The Sublime & the Beautiful*, Pier Paolo Pasolini's *'Divine' Mimesis*, and *The Selected Poems* of Emilio Villa.

For the complete list of forthcoming publications, please visit our website. To be added to our mailing list, send your name and email address to: info@contramundum.net

Contra Mundum Press
P.O. Box 1326
New York, NY 10276
USA
http://contramundum.net

OTHER CONTRA MUNDUM PRESS TITLES

Gilgamesh
Ghérasim Luca, *Self-Shadowing Prey*
Rainer J. Hanshe, *The Abdication*
Walter Jackson Bate, *Negative Capability*
Miklós Szentkuthy, *Marginalia on Casanova*
Fernando Pessoa, *Philosophical Essays*
Elio Petri, *Writings on Cinema & Life*
Friedrich Nietzsche, *The Greek Music Drama*
Richard Foreman, *Plays with Films*
Louis-Auguste Blanqui, *Eternity by the Stars*
Miklós Szentkuthy, *Towards the One & Only Metaphor*

SOME FORTHCOMING TITLES

Emilio Villa, *The Selected Poems of Emilio Villa*
Jean-Jacques Rousseau, *Narcissus*
Fernando Pessoa, *The Transformation Book*
Alfred de Vigny, *The Fates*
Miklós Szentkuthy, *Prae*
Remy de Gourmont, *The Problem of Style*

ABOUT THE AUTHOR

Josef Winkler is the author of nearly twenty books, among them the award-winning trilogy *Das wilde Kärnten*. His major themes are suicide, homosexuality, and the corrosive influence of Catholicism and Nazism in Austrian country life. Winner of the 2008 Büchner prize and current president of the Austrian Arts Senate, Winkler lives in Klagenfurt with his wife & two children.

ABOUT THE TRANSLATOR

Adrian West is a writer and literary translator from the western Romance languages and German. His work has appeared in numerous journals in print & online, including *McSweeney's*, the *Brooklyn Rail*, *Words Without Borders*, and *3:AM*. He lives with the cinema critic Beatriz Leal Riesco.

CPSIA information can be obtained at www.ICGtesting.com
Printed in the USA
LVOW04s0017291114

416147LV00018B/961/P

9 781940 625010